Time: Alternate Dimension

Teodor Singleton

Contents

PROLOGUE

- -

The world of 2490 is a wasteland. Not in the way a trashcan would look, but the way a deserted hospital would.

A place that is as dusty as the cover of a leather-bound book but has a fading memory of cleanliness and disinfectant. Like rugged concrete and gleaming white tiles.

Ryder hadn't ever seen natural green in his life, and doubted that he ever would.

His father hadn't, his mother hadn't, neither had their parents and their parents' parents. The atmosphere on Earth was so toxic now, that not even plants could survive outside without human technology.

By 2070, the Earth could no longer sustain humanity and the world fell into panic. By 2090, a new system of government had been set up and a solution was produced. The world was to stay at a population of ten billion or less for the rest of its days.

At any cost.

By 2100, the oxygen the Earth provided wasn't enough to sustain humanity any more, but by then trees were no longer needed. Humans could artificially and successfully produce the tiny atoms that they needed to survive.

In the three hundred or so years after that, Earth disintegrated into a dry, dead, shell. The air was toxic, the dirt and water was poison and humanity was dying.

But as all parasites do, humans adapted, evolved and overcame the problem.

Now relying on their own creations to survive, humans drifted through space on a withered, dead rock – descending into mindless repetition. Insanity is often described as doing something over and over again and expecting a different result to all the previous ones. And that was exactly what future humanity had laid out for itself.

Humans were parasites. Viruses even. Multiplying and feeding off their hosts until they themselves were left to die out. Every virus needs a healthy host and that was exactly what humans had until they had sucked their last victim dry.

Humanity was always destined to die like everything else in the world – it was only a question of when.

Ryder looked forward to the day that he finally passed from this world. He – just like them all – was dying, and although he wasn't quite dead yet, he couldn't help but think:

This is not a life worth living.

Chapter 1

The city looked like it was covered in mist. A heavy fog that settled over the buildings until he couldn't even see his own hand in front of his face. He'd bumped into eight people already and had only caught a glimpse of the oxygen masks over their face before they were lost to the smoke again.

Only it wasn't comforting wood smoke that wafted over grilled meat on the fire, but a choking toxin that buried itself in your lungs and spread its roots, rotting you away like candy against pearly white teeth.

Ryder adjusted his backpack straps and continued walking forward, following the green line in front of him that shone like the beam of a lighthouse through the choking pollution – leading him home.

He smoothly avoided buildings and miraculously – people – and in an instant, the green line stopped in a swirling circle on the metal door in front of him.

Like a prison door.

Only that this one led out to a life of empty walls and closed doors, not freedom.

He tapped in the keycode, swung it open and stepped inside, closing it behind him and typing in another keycode on the opposite door. He braced himself as the air whipped around him, swirling out through the vents. "Oxygen levels are secure." The robotic voice was followed by a hiss as the door in front of him swung open and he stepped inside, closing it behind him.

"Mum?" He dropped his bag on the floor and walked through another doorway, flicking the small locks open on either side of the mask and sliding it off. "Mum?" he called again, louder this time.

"I'm in the kitchen," came a quiet voice from the other side of the house. He made his way over, sliding out of the spacesuit-like clothing he wore, and hanging it up on one of the hooks on his way.

Lana Davis was an Egyptian beauty with golden skin and wavy black hair that framed her sharp jaw and wide shoulders. At the age of forty-six, she was beautiful in a foreboding way. With a classic hourglass shape and soft skin, she caught many of her co-workers' eyes.

Ryder knew why she didn't want to remarry, but after 20 years, he thought she might be ready to let someone into her life that wasn't her son.

Artificial sunlight streaming from the ceiling and glittered on Ryder's skin.

It was the only sunlight his body had ever received.

"My job gave me a new office," she said quietly, brushing his curly black hair away from his face. This wasn't something to be congratulated about. "We're going to be moving to Hong Kong central."

"How much will it cost?" he murmured, leaning his hip against the counter.

"Three years-worth of our oxygen supply." His eyes widened.

"Can't you decline? It would take two years alone to replenish that amount in our tank account."

"I'm afraid I can't risk losing my job. Hong Kong is one of the main oxygen suppliers, so hopefully, I'll get higher pay. You'll have to resign from your job tomorrow – we're leaving the day after."

"I'll find a job in Hong Kong, don't worry mum." She put a hand on his cheek and smiled into his eyes.

"I know." She kissed his cheek right next to his nose and pushed off the counter, walking towards their shared room. "You should probably start packing tonight."

He stood there for a few moments, before walking the other way. "I'm going out for dinner with Mark, by the way, I forgot to tell you."

"Be back by eight," she called and he slid his suit back on, sealing it up and grabbing his mask, sliding it on and locking it into place.

He looked back to make sure his mother wasn't watching, then grabbed a bag from a shelf by the door, hooked it over one shoulder and disappeared into the airlock.

Once he was outside, he blinked rapidly in the sudden swirling darkness and reached for the GPS on the wristband of his suit. He tapped on one of the most searched locations and a green light lit up in front of him along the lines that led around the city.

He hated going outside his home. The last of humanity, stumbling around blinded by their own doing. It was humiliating.

Sometimes Ryder wondered if his ancestors were laughing at them all.

He trudged along the road like a machine – one foot in front of the other in a rhythmic beat that he did so subconsciously that he could follow the line perfectly while letting his mind wander, without even breaking his stride.

It was then that he was knocked flat to the ground with the wind knocked out of him.

He struggled against the person's hold, the light below him flickering and illuminating the oxygen mask in front of him in an eerie glow of green. And the object they held aloft in their right hand.

Ryder writhed in their hold as the person struggled to pin him down with only one arm while the other held the rusted knife poised to strike.

He'd heard of their kind before. Criminals – those who could no longer afford the oxygen that paid for their food and kept them alive. They survived solely by robbing people of their oxygen tanks and leaving them for dead.

Which was why this one was aiming for the valve that connected the tanks on his back to his mask.

The figure brought the knife down and he jerked to the side, flinging his attacker off his stomach and onto the ground. He stumbled to his feet, but was brought back down again with a blade slicing past his mask as he squirmed.

They rolled him onto his back and pinned him down, raising the knife once again.

He quickly snapped his body to the left and the blade crashed right through his mask and shattered the glass, slicing open his cheek.

He roared with pain and his attacker fled, leading Ryder to flail on the ground as red lights flashed all over his suit. The knife was barely keeping the right pressure in his suit, but every time he moved, it dug deeper into his cheek until he was forced to rip it out of its position halfway through his helmet.

He held his breath and put his fingers over the cracks, but the hole was too large.

His tank cut off the supply of oxygen to his mask in order to save as much of the precious gas as possible, but left Ryder to stumble to his feet and blindly search for a repair station.

Like ATM's, oxygen and repair stations were built everywhere and allowed for damaged suits, helmets and tanks to be repaired or replenished – paid for by the amount of oxygen you earned and saved in your tank account.

But with his fingers fumbling at the GPS and his vision going blurry, Ryder was in no state to be able to find such a station and was left to crumple to the ground, eyes glazing over as he gagged on the pollution that streamed into his mask.

A figure leaned over his body and he felt himself being turned onto his side. He didn't and couldn't fight back. They'd come back for the tank.

His mask was ripped off and the toxins swirled before his eyes.

Ryder opened his mouth to scream for help, but a hand was slapped over his mouth and nose.

Then something was slid over his head and locked into place and he gulped in glorious air.

His fuzzy vision tried to focus on the figure hovering above him, but all he could see was their blurry oxygen mask at the edge of his vision before he finally blacked out.

Waking was painful. The light that attacked his eyelids stung his eyes and brought tears to stream through the gaps. His head throbbed, his throat burned and his body felt like stone. He'd heard of sleep paralysis before, but had never experienced it. "Don't try to move," a voice said from his left.

He tried to crane his neck towards it, but he couldn't.

Ryder began to panic.

"Don't try to move, speak, or even think. I promise that I am not here to hurt you. Try to let yourself relax back into unconsciousness – it will be easier the next time you wake." He struggled to move for a while longer, before finally giving up. "That's it," he heard the voice come from above him – soft, feminine and reassuring.

He let himself drift away, and true to their word, the next time he woke, he could open his eyes without any trouble at all.

It was darker than last time, and he could feel the familiar weight of a blanket over his body and it brushed against his chin as he moved his head from side to side, trying to get a glimpse of his surroundings.

He was definitely in a hospital, but the walls weren't made of concrete, glass or white ceramic tiles – but what looked like pure, rugged stone.

And lining the stone walls were wooden torches of fire.

His eyes boggled and he struggled to sit up, which obviously set off some sort of alarm because after his heart monitor hit the ceiling, someone came rushing into the room wearing pale lilac robes. "No no no, don't mess with those," the woman scolded, slapping his hands away from the small scalpels he was reaching for to arm himself with.

"Who are you and where am I?" he demanded, gripping the white bedsheets so tight his knuckles turned the same shade. "And are you crazy putting those things up!?" he gestured to the flames flickering along the walls. "Especially in a hospital! You're tossing money down the drain, you do realise?" The woman chuckled and tucked him into bed to his annoyance, completely disregarding his struggling and calmly instructing him to lie back down.

"Where you are now – doesn't require people to pay for basic things they need to survive."

"So you're saying you don't have to pay for the oxygen you're wasting right now?" He snorted. "Where am I then, Venus?"

"Rest. My Lady will come to explain once you are well."

"Why can't this lady come and speak to me now?" he snapped.

"Rest," she repeated softly, plumping up another pillow and tucking it under his head so he could sit up slightly, which successfully cleared his blocked nose.

"Fine," he sulked like a child and she nodded.

"I'll get you a glass of water."

Reality slapped him in the face and he shot upright. "Wait!"

She turned. "Yes, darling?"

"Can you contact my mum? To make sure she knows I'm okay?" The woman smiled softly at him.

"Certainly. What's her name?"

"Lana Catherina Davis." She nodded, turned and walked out the door, leaving Ryder to his own thoughts. She only came back to hand him a glass of water and to place a jug beside him to fill it up by himself.

After lying there for quite some time, staring at the flames with his fingers twitching, Ryder finally got up and stumbled over to them with his glass of water in hand.

He threw it over the first flame and leapt back in surprise when it roared even louder and flamed blindingly bright, before settling back down to its original flame.

He stood dumbfounded for a moment, before teetering over to the bed and sliding into the sheets with his eyes still the size of saucers and staring blankly at the ceiling. About an hour later, the door opened and closed and he jerked abruptly out of his stupor. "Is my mum coming to –" His eyes fell on the figure who had stopped by the foot of his bed and he shrunk underneath the bedsheets.

The woman towered above him, her back straight and shoulders back, her ice-blue eyes staring down at him, void of any emotion. She looked far more athletic than the previous woman, with a slim yet strong figure that was covered in heavy black armour, trimmed with gold.

Her face was covered in a mask adorned with spikes, leaving only her eyes to bore into his.

"Your mother has been contacted and will be able to visit you as soon as we are able to arrange it," she said smoothly, still standing as straight and stiff as a plank of wood.

"O-okay," he cleared his throat and almost withered under her gaze.

"My name is Una," she said, walking over to his bedside and sitting down in the chair beside him in one fluid movement, that had Ryder wondering if she even had bones at all. "Just like everyone else here, however you shall address me as 'My Lady' or 'Lady Una.'" He nodded, still squirming under her stare.

She crossed one leg over the other and leaned back in the chair before reaching up to the back of her neck.

She peeled the two sides away from her skin and pulled the mask off her face, placing it on her lap and running one hand through her loose, black hair.

She was distinctly Eurasian and as she shifted in her seat he noticed she had a pair of golden rings in the cartilage of her left ear.

"You're probably wondering where you are and why you are here, and the simple answer to that is you are in a different world. Why you are here is because your father is one of my trusted advisors and requested you be brought here instead of perishing in your crumbling human world." He sat in awkward silence with her gaze boring into him.

"And the complex answer is?" he managed to force out. To his surprise she cracked a smile, which widened into a grin, then exploded into roaring laughter that had him wishing he would just disappear into the mattress.

"Oh you humans do amuse me," she said humorously, before standing abruptly. "Hayleen," she called to the open door before turning back to him. "She will find you some appropriate clothing and then you shall come with me, but only if she deems you fit to do so."

"Why?" he finally dared to ask and she grinned maliciously.

"You did ask for the complex answer." Then she strode away.

Ryder let out a loud breath, flopping back onto the pillows behind him and running a hand over his face. "What did you get yourself into this time?" he muttered before the woman from earlier came rushing over with a stack of neatly folded clothes.

She bustled him through the door like a mother hen and stripped him of his hospital gown to which Ryder began blushing profusely, but being a supposed doctor or nurse, Hayleen didn't skip a beat and continued pushing his legs through the army-green track pants, buttoning up his shirt, slipping his arms through a jacket and zipping it all the way up to his collar.

She dusted off his shoulders and he cleared his throat to get her attention. "Um, thanks, I guess," he mumbled and she beamed so brightly he couldn't help but give her a flustered smile back.

"Are you decent?" came a voice from outside and the woman bustled him out again with a bright 'yes, his is My Lady.'

He shifted from foot to foot, feeling inadequate in his casual clothing next to her metal battledress.

"This way," she said, gliding down the hallway and he rushed after her.

"So my father is your... Advisor?"

"Correct." He licked his lips and struggled to fall into step with her.

"My father's still alive?"

"Of course."

"But surely you know when a child is born one of their parents has to be... reaped, if there are no volunteers in order to keep the population stable?"

"Yes. Which is why your parents chose your father to be killed, because he came from this world, not the one you grew up in. We simply took him back to this one after he was supposedly 'killed' but all we had to do was trick the machines into thinking they had burned the right body, when in fact it was a fake." He tried to digest the information and that's when it clicked.

"That's why my mother never remarried, isn't it. Because she knew that my father was still alive."

"Correct." She turned to him with gleaming eyes. "You catch on quickly. I'm surprised you believed me instantly when I said we weren't in your world anymore." He shrugged.

"I've always wanted to leave. So if this is a dream, I'm going to hang onto it for as long as I can." He frowned at the ground for a while. "But how can there be another world? Are we on another planet? Are we underground? Maybe a parallel universe?"

"No to the first two, but you're pretty much right on the third. We live on a higher plane to your world, which is practically a parallel universe anyway."

"Wicked," he breathed quietly and he could have sworn her mouth twitched into a smile at that, but there was no way she could have heard him.

She stopped at a door on the left and put her hand on the handle, turning to him before she opened it. "Do you think you're ready to meet your father?"

"No," he said firmly and she raised an eyebrow slightly at his tone.

"But?" she prodded and he shrugged his shoulders.

"But let's do it," he said and she pushed open the door.

A massive table was set up in the room in half a doughnut shape. It curved around the edges of the room and around fifty chairs lined the outer edge, with only four people sitting in the very middle. Two males and two females.

And when the male on the far right stood, their eyes locked and Ryder pretty much wanted to sprint over and hug the living daylights out of him.

Right after he'd punched him square in the nose.

"Go on," Una said, gesturing to the table and Ryder slowly walked over, while his father stepped through a gap and did the same.

They met in the middle of the room and Ryder stared at him.

He was a brawny Egyptian man with a rough beard and an uneven scar down the side of his head where his thick black hair was unable to grow.

He was taller and larger than Ryder and apart from their near-identical faces, the only other features they shared were their curly black hair and chocolate brown eyes.

The man cleared his throat and rubbed the back of his neck. "Hi, uh... Son," he said before coughing and clearing his throat again.

"Way to go, Jarred," the second male's voice teased from the table. The skin on his cheeks and the bridge of his nose turned darker.

"Shut it," he growled and Ryder couldn't help but chuckle a little.

"Hey, dad." Then he wrapped his arms around his shoulders and tugged him into a death grip.

He stood frozen for a few moments before returning the hug and patting Ryder on the back.

"Thank goodness, I thought you were going to punch me," he whistled and Ryder grinned.

"Oh I am, but I'm going to wait until I'm as big as you before I do, so it'll hurt like hell."

"That's your boy all right," one of the women cheered. "Do me a favour and get it on video would ya?" she winked at Ryder and he grinned.

"Definitely."

He turned and saw Una staring into the distance with a faraway look, before nodding and turning to him. "Loch Ness has arranged for your mother to see you two in a week's time. Because of Ryder's 'death,' they're suspending her trip until the coming Tuesday. That's when we can sabotage the ship and fake her death."

"Does she know I'm alive?" Ryder blurted and she nodded.

"She's fully aware of what's going to happen and is already arranging for all your belongings to be on the ship with her so we can collect everything when we get there." She looked at Ryder, then his father, then back again.

"Jarred, Loch Ness just requested for you to be released from your duties for the rest of the day. She says..." Una's face went strange. "'Spend some time with your son and for the love of everything good in this world don't set the palace on fire again.'"

"Yes Milady," he said with a sheepish grin and Ryder almost screamed.

"You set a palace on fire!?" he hissed as soon as they were out of earshot.

"A while ago," he said gloomily.

"That's awesome how on Earth did you do it?" He gave Ryder a stunned grin, checked around for anyone within earshot, then leaned in and whispered:

"In this world, there are creatures and even people that you can't believe. I'm not actually classified as human – I'm an elemental."

"No way. Like those weird witchy people who can use one of the four elements?"

"Yep. And guess which one I am?" Ryder was almost bursting with excitement.

"But how did you manage to set an entire building on fire!?" He chuckled.

"One day I'll teach you." Ryder was suddenly hit by the most incredible thought that made him dizzy just imagining it.

"Am I a fire elemental too?" Jarred's face fell and he turned away.

"No. A human and elemental can't have hybrid children – they're always human."

"Oh," Ryder said in disappointment. They walked in silence for a few moments. "You can still teach me the old fashioned way though right?" his father grinned and the both of them chatted on their way down the hall, laughing like old pals all the way.

Ryder decided that he'd let his mother yell at him for abandoning the two of them for twenty years. Ryder personally thought there wasn't much point in holding a grudge against him – he wanted to spend as much time with his as possible to make up for the lost twenty years of his life.

His father showed him to his new room in the student quarters and the two of them lounged on the bed as Jarred began to explain to Ryder what that realm was like.

"You wouldn't believe me if I told you," was the first thing he'd said when Ryder asked about it. "You'll have to see it for yourself." And since then, he'd been dying to experience it for himself.

His father answered as many questions as he could and Ryder learned that the leaders were royalty – descended by blood – but in some rare cases the leaders were chosen and the bloodlines of the royal family were changed.

The last time that had happened was seven centuries ago.

Despite how cold and vague Una acted towards him, Ryder was curious to as what her role was as a royal.

Jarred explained that she was the second-born child of three and that their mother had died in a battle for the freedom of Earth. A few years later their father died and the firstborn child turned tail and bolted as soon as they realised they would become the leader.

So at the age of seven, Una had been crowned the leader of the Kediotherylan realm. Being born and taught to be royalty is one thing, but being hammered into the role of a queen is something completely different. So onward from her eighth birthday, Una was taught everything it took to be a perfect leader, but never did she have a role model to show her how to be a good one.

Her story intrigued Ryder and so he had asked about the first born child. His father had simply said that they had run off and he knew nothing more of what had happened to them.

But what really drew him in was when he asked about the younger sibling.

His father had said that the child was never born – their mother having died while eight months pregnant with them. However, when Ryder asked why his father had said Una was one of three siblings if only two had ever been alive, he had slammed the door to the answer in his face and strictly told him to never ask him about it again.

After a moment of tense silence, Jarred had apologised and mentioned that it was a sensitive topic for many of them, especially Una and gave him a warning to never mention it in front of her.

Ryder took to nodding, but noting in his head to find out what his mind found so suspicious about the third royal's story and to settle the churning in his stomach.

With Lady Una's permission, Jarred was allowed to take Ryder outside the student living quarters and let him experience the elemental realm.

And like his father had said, Ryder couldn't even believe what he was seeing in front of his own eyes.

The moment he stepped out of the door he was hit by blinding, dazzling sunlight that glittered over a vast terrain of green that Ryder couldn't see the end of.

Animals and even people walked around freely in the sun without the need for oxygen masks and Ryder was completely stunned.

"Welcome to paradise," his father chuckled, slapping him on the back and he grinned widely, still staring out over the river valley that stretched further than he could see.

Creatures – the only word for what he was seeing – frolicked in the grass and the river winding between the two mountain ranges. There were horses with six legs and manes made of fire and deer twice their size. What looked like a Griffin stood on a rock, hunches in the air and wings folded at its sides before it launched itself at one of the deer and brought it down in a single swipe of its talons. A few people walked near the river and Ryder saw a group of them sparring together, with one pair in particular piquing his interest. Fire burst from the female's palms and the male used his fists to bring up walls of rock. Massive buildings were carved out of the mountains with greenery surrounding it and making most of them almost disappear into the landscape.

"Whoa," he breathed, vowing that if it truly was a dream, he'd remember it for eternity.

They were standing on a rocky ledge carved out of the mountainside, around a hundred feet above the ground.

Ryder yelled and jumped back from the edge as something four times the size of a double-decker bus glided right past him.

It had what looked a little like a hawk's head except the 'feathers' around its face was actually smooth and shiny like polished bone. Ryder realised it was actually a thick armoured plate like some dragons had in storybooks. The rest of it was covered in fur and it had a wolf-like body and what seemed like a peacock's tail swishing behind it.

Its wings were also covered in gleaming blue and green feathers – the shortest of which was probably twice Ryder's height.

His jaw just about hit the floor.

"That one's just a baby," his father grinned. "Wait till you see its mother."

"No thanks," he said quickly and watched as it swung around and glided back towards them, landing on a ledge above the two.

It bent its neck over the edge and stared down at Ryder as he craned his neck up to look at it.

Both of its massive golden eyes looked directly at him and he gulped, rendered speechless by the sheer size of it.

Then what looked like a vertical golden oval in between its two eyes opened, revealing a third.

It was pitch black and Ryder couldn't help but feel like it was staring right into him, but then it closed and the creature jumped off the ledge and soared away.

"They're very ancient creatures – one of the first supernatural beings to have shaped this realm," his father said quietly. "Its third eye only opens when it wants to see into someone, to see their past, their strengths and weaknesses and their intentions."

"That's creepy," Ryder shivered and his father put a hand on his shoulder, eyes serious.

"They also only look at people with their spiritual eye when they are either a royal, someone very dangerous, someone unusual or special or even all three of those together."

"Well, are they many humans here?" Ryder asked and his father's eyes flicked to the ledge below them.

"Not many."

"Maybe that's it then. Besides, it's a baby – it was probably just testing its supernatural powers out." His father grunted in agreement and rolled his shoulders.

"Want to go down there?" Ryder snorted.

"What do you think?"

Chapter 2

<hr>

"So how was your first day in the Kediotherylan realm?" Ryder barked out a laugh as he walked down the hall with his father to the student dining room.

"It means that you're not human."

"Awesome," he grinned and Jarred pushed the doors open.

Loud laughter and chatter blasted Ryder in the face as soon as the doors swung open and he stumbled back slightly, his eyes wide.

Hundreds of people sat in long benches down the room, ages varying from around five to – well, they looked fifty, but Ryder knew better. His father had told him some elementals could live for centuries.

"You can sit up at the front with me until you make some friends," he said and Ryder glared. "What?" he asked, eyes widening.

"Nothing, nothing." They wandered through the gaps between the tables, with people calling 'Advisor Jarred,' with a bow of their head in respect as they passed and Ryder stuck to his father's side with his head down.

When they reached the table, his father dragged a chair over and Ryder sat at the edge of the table.

Una sat in the middle with a female on either side of her, then Jarred and the other male on either side of them.

Their table was higher than all the others, and directly below them – halfway up the steps – was another table with five people seated at it.

"Who are they?" he whispered to his father as soon as he'd finished bowing to Una with a 'My Lady.'

"That's Lady Una's best team of senior students," he replied, digging into the – was it beef? Ryder couldn't tell – on his plate. "Each team must have at least one of every element because they work stronger that way. Earth is the most powerful element when it is shared, but is weak on its own, as all the others can only alter nature to their will but –"

"What?" His father pushed his chair closer with a shrill squeak and leaned towards him.

"Earth elementals can manipulate plants, earth, rocks – you name it. Anything natural, they can handle – but only if it already exists. Right?"

"Yeah..."

"Well, the fire and water elementals can make this power stronger. Water elementals can cause mudslides and nurture plants to grow tougher and larger at will. On top of this, they can also manipulate water itself. Fire elementals can manipulate fire, but not only does earth give them a substance to burn and nurture the flame, but if you combine heat with certain ores – you get metal."

"And earth elementals can't do this by themselves?"

"No. Earth is the weakest element, but if fire and water wish to become stronger, an earth elemental basically amplifies their power."

"Okay... What about air elementals?"

"Air elementals have been mistaken for the most powerful element for years, because they are completely separate to the others," Jarred explained, waving his fork around. "They don't rely on earth to make their power stronger – they rely on each other. That's why air elementals always travel in pairs. You see those two males there?" He pointed at the table with his fork and Ryder saw the two men dressed in grey uniforms. "See how there is only one of every other element?"

Sitting with them were two females – one in blood red and another in army green.

The third wore black – but Ryder assumed they were a water elemental.

"So the other two rely on the one in green, but the two in grey amplify their power in numbers?"

"Precisely." He nodded and squinted.

"Who is that, by the way? The figure in black?"

"Call sign – Loch Ness," Jarred replied. "People call her Lochy – the youngest teacher at the academy."

"Male or female? And why are they wearing a mask?" Unlike the other four at the table, the figure wasn't eating and wore a black helmet similar to a motorcycle one – except you could only see through one way and the sides were adorned with spikes.

"Female. She suffered from a fierce blow to the head with elemental fire as a child – she almost lost her eyesight, but we were able to repair her eyes. Her face was unable to heal completely and is deformed." Ryder winced in empathy and no longer asked about her.

He couldn't help but stare at the table of elementals the whole night though, watching them all chat and laugh together – even the girl in black.

Halfway through the dinner however, they all walked up to their table and Loch Ness knelt down in front of Una.

She rose and so did her four advisors, leaving Ryder perched halfway out of his seat, unsure whether he should do the same.

Una nodded to the girl, who stood and bowed her head. "You requested I see you for our next mission, My Lady?" Her voice was quiet, but by no means soft.

"Yes, I have decided that you will be put with several other senior water elementals, to train them and command them for a mission to the Dead Sea."

The other four members all began complaining at the same time, which left Ryder a little shocked at how they talked to their leader.

To his surprise, Una seemed used to it and firmly explained that 'No, you can't go with her cause none of you can breathe underwater you morons' – well she didn't exactly say that, but her tone suggested it.

"Yes, My Lady," they grumbled.

The girl in red seemed the most bothered by it, and crossed her arms with a fierce pout.

"Good," the royal said in satisfaction. "I will assign Natalie to be your temporary water elemental –"

They all started complaining again.

Una sighed and put a hand over her face and Jarred stepped in. "It's just for a week guys, surely you can all –"

"A week!?" they all shrieked and Ryder stepped back in surprise.

"She leaves tomorrow," Una said, looking sternly at each of them in turn.

"If I may, My Lady," Loch Ness interrupted, "I was to supervise Zachary in the hospital tomorrow night, is it possible for the date to be moved to Thursday?"

"Isn't your shift tonight?"

"Yes."

"But if you left on Thursday that would mean you'd be deprived of three days and two nights worth of sleep – you'd be in no shape to lead the mission."

"I could attempt quiet energy preservation on the ship."

"I'm afraid I cannot take that risk, Loch Ness. If you went under, you could be for a long time."

"I understand," the masked woman said quietly.

"I will supervise Zachary myself if you wish," Una offered and Loch Ness roared with laughter.

Ryder gave his father a wide-eyed look.

He shrugged as if this was a daily occurrence.

"I am sorry My Lady, that's a very generous offer, thank you." Una's lips tilted into a small smile that had Ryder gaping like a beached fish.

He had no clue she was capable of any emotion other than scorn and grim humour.

"You are worried he'd be too embarrassed to take up my offer." It was a statement.

"I will ensure he is notified, don't worry," Loch Ness assured, then bowed and waited for Una's call.

"Dismissed," she said with a wave of her hand and the woman nodded her head, then descended down the stairs with her team trailing after her.

Everyone sat back down again and Una resumed talking to the air elemental female beside her.

"Well that was certainly something," Ryder stated. "How are they all allowed to talk to her that way? I've seen her with other elementals and they're terrified of her." Jarred seemed to think about what he was going to say for a moment.

"My Lady doesn't have many... Friends. To rule is to be lonely – not many people can even give you suggestions and you're expected to treat everyone as if they are below you. Since all of her immediate family died or in her sibling's case – left – Una had been surrounded by people more than thrice her age and the closest relationship they had was one a student would have with their teacher. As all royals do, she was gifted by the ability to learn things uncannily fast and as soon as she became a teacher, she took Loch Ness up as her first and only student after her parents abandoned her because of her damaged face. She grew to become the finest student they had ever had and is nearing the skill of her current teachers – the finest in the whole realm. Una has a certain respect for Loch Ness that one would only find in extremely close friendships. Some people might even go as far as to say that they are friends.

"She treats Loch Ness like her equal, but she must still call Lady Una by her formal title, and if she gives Loch Ness a direct order – she must obey like everyone else."

"Wow," he mumbled, glancing up at Una.

She had the highest spot in the room, her chair elevated slightly compared to everyone else's, which showed her status.

"What about the rest of the team?" Jarred smiled.

"Una has very specific respect and trust in her student. Those who Loch Ness trusts with her life and respects like an equal – so does she."

"That's a... pretty strong friendship," he forced out pathetically.

"It is. But there are many like that here – it's simply unusual for royalty to have one. One day you'll find someone or even more than one person – whom you trust with your life and respect like they are equal to you in every way, even if they aren't in the world's pecking order.

"And if you're lucky – very lucky – you might even get the chance to work with all of them for the rest of your life."

"You're referring to a team, aren't you," Ryder said with a raised eyebrow. Jarred sighed.

"Just because you're human, doesn't mean you won't find –"

"I never said anything about me being human," Ryder said with his hands up in surrender.

"But you know what you meant," he said with both eyebrows raised.

Ryder assumed that was where he got his expressive eyebrows from.

"Oh alright, fine. I know that I won't get a team, because one, I'm human, two, I don't understand this world or how it works yet, and three, I'm still waiting to wake up and find myself in a trashcan of a planet, with you dead and a nurse telling me I was in a coma for several years after someone tried to stab me." He took a deep breath in after his rant and his father chuckled.

"Ryder, you're not dreaming, I assure you –"

"That's what my dream brain would make my dream characters say."

He was suddenly punched in the shoulder so hard he was pummelled straight out of his chair.

"What was that for!?" He shrieked as soon as his backside hit the floor and he heard Scott guffawing at him from the other end of the table.

"Did that feel real?" his father snickered.

"You could have just pinched me or something," he scowled, pulling his chair back upright and slumping in it.

"Nah, it wouldn't have been as funny then."

"You should have seen your face!" Scott laughed and Ryder glared until he stopped, wiping tears from his eyes and grinning like a madman.

Una suddenly stood and gestured for her advisors to stay seated, then left.

"Where's she going?" Ryder whispered to his father as Una walked past and she stopped, turning to him with icy eyes.

He squeaked in fear on instinct and Scott lost it at the other side of the table.

"I'm capable of speaking for myself you know," Una said slowly and Ryder nodded with a flustered,

"Yes, sorry My Lady."

"I'm going to see Loch Ness and her team, then I'm going to see my teachers, train and then retreat to my quarters – any questions on my personal life?" She didn't snap at him at all, just said it in such a calm and serene voice that had Ryder trying to fold back into his chair.

"No!" he squeaked and she nodded, then her lips lifted into a smug smirk that made him flush a deep, dark red.

"Good night, Ryder Davis," she called over her shoulder, then walked down the stairs and towards the door at the other side of the dining hall.

He let out a relieved breath and sat back upright in his chair.

"She's definitely terrifying, and there's nothing you can say or do that will make me change my mind," he said firmly.

His father smiled slightly.

"I can't, but maybe she will."

Dinner ended with Ryder attempting to make his way back to his quarters by himself.

His father had things to attend to and Scott had offered, but Ryder had declined. He had told the advisor he'd like to see some air manipulation the next time he saw him and the brown-haired man had agreed, telling Ryder he'd arrange it with Una and Loch Ness.

After a short talk about Una, he'd left Ryder to wander back to his dorm.

According to what Scott and Jarred had told him, Loch Ness was basically Una's student, secretary and advisor all in one. Not only that, but she was the realm's head elemental-specialised doctor and inventor of all their weapons and armour.

Ryder hated to think of all the things Una had to do.

"Hey, are you lost?" he whipped around and saw a woman with her hand on the door handle, smiling at him gently.

"Well – kind of?"

"If you can remember what room number your dorm is, I can take you there. I just got back from training, so I have plenty of free time before bed."

"Oh! No it's okay, I wouldn't want to bother you, I'm sure I can find it myself," he chuckled nervously, but she closed the door, locked it and walked over with a soft laugh.

"Trust me, it's fine." She was Eurasian just like Una, but her hair was brown and her eyes were more almond shape and smaller than hers. She didn't look much like Una at all, but it was plain their race was similar.

"I actually don't remember the number," Ryder winced, wondering how he even thought he'd be able to find it without someone's help.

"That's okay," she said breezily. "What species are you?" He was a little taken aback, but managed a muttered,

"Uh, human." Her eyes widened and her mouth broke out into a huge grin.

"Oh you're Advisor Jarred's boy, aren't you?" She grabbed his hand and shook it warmly. "It's really an honour to finally meet you!"

"I – what?" she put her lips by his ear and whispered

"In my opinion, your dad's the best advisor of all of them."

"Really?"

"Yeah!" she flicked her hair behind her shoulder with a grin. "Apart from Scott of course – he's practically everyone's dad. Actually no – Jarred's everyone's dad, Scott's the crazy uncle that leaves the stove on and sets the house on fire. Oh, wait no your dad's the fire elemental – never mind." She suddenly gasped and put one hand over her mouth and one on his shoulder. "Oh my god, I'm so sorry! That was really insensitive of me saying that when he hasn't been around for you..."

"Oh no, it's fine," he said with a smile, mind still whirring at the whole load of information she just threw at him. "Anyway, I'm Ryder." He stuck his hand out and even though she's already shaken his hand and knew his name, she did it again.

"Natalie."

"Oh! So you're Loch Ness's replacement?" Before he could apologise for how forward he was, her face lit up.

"Yes, I am!" She sighed, staring into the distance with a blissful smile on her face. "I can't believe Una chose me – I mean I'm not even one of the top seniors!"

"Well, congratulations."

"Thanks!" She walked around with him for a while, enjoying each other's company as they searched for his room.

"How old are you? I mean, it's okay you don't have to answer if –"

"I'm nineteen," she said with a smile. "You?"

"I'm twenty. Nineteen and you're already Loch Ness's replacement?" She gave him a knowing smile as if she knew something he didn't and he frowned slightly.

"Yeah, I guess. Not meaning to brag or anything, but I learn faster than most people, so that's probably why I was chosen."

"So you're a water elemental right? Can you show me something?" She nodded.

"What do you want to see?"

"Well – uh, anything really." She put her hand up and after a few seconds, water beaded on Ryder's skin and slid off, darting to her palm and conjoining into a levitating ball of water the size of a small marble. "Whoa," he breathed.

She put her hand up so both palms were facing each other, and moved her fingers in a way that made the droplet move from side to side, bouncing off her skin.

She let it soak back into his skin and he stood there dumbstruck for a moment.

"That was... wow," he forced out, shaking his head and she smiled.

"If you think that's cool, you should see what Lady Una can do."

"Oh right, she's a water elemental too, right?" She shook her head.

"Not quite. Royals are gifted with a second power that relates to their first. Una can not only control water, but she is the only person in this realm who can also control ice."

"What about her sibling? You know, the one that ran off?"

Her expression darkened almost immediately and her eyes flicked to the wall.

"We don't speak of them here," she said in a low voice and he swallowed awkwardly.

"Hey! I recognise this hallway." He said suddenly, stopping. She turned to him.

"Really?"

"Yeah, my room's just around that corner. Thanks for helping me by the way,"

"No problem," she said with a small smile. "I'll see you around?"

"Sure." She waved and walked down the hallway, leaving Ryder in the middle of the academy.

He'd lied.

He had no idea where he was, but at least he'd have time to ponder her reaction in silence.

He shrugged, put his hands in his pockets and continued to walk down the hall.

The doors were further apart than the others, and each door had a symbol on it that he hadn't seen before.

He looked at each as he passed – a dagger, a moon, a corked bottle and an empty circle.

He turned to walk back the other way when he heard a shriek from the door beside him.

He walked towards it and leaned close, hearing a muffled male voice screeching from inside.

"No way. No – I won't allow it. No, no, no and no." The second voice was softer and Ryder ended up with his ear against the wood to hear them.

"Well, you don't exactly have much choice."

"Get someone else to do it! I'm sure Meredith can –"

"Meredith hasn't been to the academy in eight days – you know this. And she doesn't have any medical experience."

"She's been alive the past nine centuries, I'm sure she's picked up some extensive knowledge." Ryder heard an audible sigh.

"Look –" their voice was cut off suddenly and there was silence for a few seconds. "You can come in you know Ryder – that's what doors are for."

He slowly pushed the door open and stood sheepishly in the doorway.

Loch Ness stood by a large wooden table with one hand on its polished surface and the other up with her gloved palm facing the man in front of her, as if she had put her hand up to stop him from speaking.

She probably had.

The large spiked helmet turned to him, it's sleek black surface revealing nothing of her facial features. "I see you've found the elemental medical room – I assume you're lost?" He narrowed his eyes.

"What makes you say that?"

"Because your dorm is on the other side of the academy, it's been two hours since dinner ended, and you can't do elemental training, so there's no need for you to see me." He shrugged.

"Fair enough."

"You can come in if you want and wait until I'm done – then I can show you to your room." He opened his mouth to argue, but gave up and closed the door behind him. "This is Zachary – my apprentice."

"Hey," the man waved, flicking his brown hair out of his face.

"You have an apprentice? I thought you were Una's student."

"So Jarred told you," she mused aloud. "Yes, but everyone has a teacher and a student. It's a complicated system, but within a year you'll know exactly where you and everyone else sits in the 'pecking order.'

"Una is taught by Meredith and Marcus, who are the finest elementals in the known realm. They taught Una, who taught me. I now learn from them too, but unlike Una, I have many students, who in turn have students and so forth."

"Kinda makes sense." Zachary looked older than him, but was shorter than Loch Ness and taller than Ryder.

"Hey, would you mind if I did a check-up?"

"On me?" Zach nodded. "There aren't many humans here and I've never been able to get one in here before."

"Uh, I guess? What kind of check-up do you mean?"

"I just want to see how humans work," he said with a smile.

"I've told you this before – humans are just like us, but with a limited amount of internal energy," Loch Ness said impatiently. He pouted childishly.

"I know, but it's still interesting!"

"I'm fine with it, honestly," Ryder reassured and the woman sighed, putting her hand over her helmet.

"Alright fine." Zachary clenched his fist with a hissed 'Yes!' and hurried Ryder over to a large table in the middle of the room. "I'll be in my room, call me if you need me – I need to finish up some potions before I take you to your room," she said to the two of them and they nodded.

She disappeared out the door and Ryder was helped onto the table.

It had a metal rim and was rectangular in shape, and hollowed out in the middle. Small lights dotted the rim and when Zach flicked them on, they all crisscrossed the air just above the bottom of the shallow box-like structure in a blue grid.

"Just lay right on top of the lights," he instructed and Ryder clambered into the space, lying down on the cold metal surface and letting the lights hit his body. "Stay as still as you can." The lights began moving over his body and his eyes flicked down to his chest and saw the blue grid engulfing his frame until he looked much like the computerised human figures used in simulations.

He felt himself being lifted up until he was slightly above the table at Zachary's hip height.

"Don't try to move – you'll find you won't be able to until the lights turn off anyway. Just relax and close your eyes."

Ryder obeyed and felt his heart rate slowly return to normal.

"Good... good.. good," he heard Zach mutter from beside him. He was jabbed lightly in the waist and he choked out a laugh, trying to shy away, but finding he was frozen. "Sorry," Zach chuckled, then his tone darkened with an "Oh."

There were a few beeps and he heard him muttering as he typed something. "Holy Shit," he exclaimed and Ryder opened his eyes to try and look in his direction as he heard loud footsteps thundering away with a yelled "LOCH NESS!!"

The door opened and closed and he saw Loch Ness's spiked helmet hover above him. "Look at the scan."

"My god," she murmured and began typing something on the keyboard beside Ryder's head. "You'll be able to move your head now, but nothing else."

He nodded and found himself actually being able to – then turned to face her.

She held up a glass rectangle in front of his face, tilting it so he could see. "Do you know what this is?" He squinted at the screen, which had a faint blue outline of a human body, with a gold background that filled the screen.

"It that me?"

"Yes, but do you know what that is?" She pointed right in the middle of the scan.

"Me??" he repeated, baffled.

"We took several scans, and since this is an elemental scanner it automatically took one of your internal energy. Humans have a limited amount and can't stream it into an element in order to manipulate it. This is the chart of a normal human." She flicked the image to one of a similar body shape, with a black background and a golden pinprick of light in the brain, the heart and the crotch.

She zoomed in and showed him the fireball-looking circles in the scan. "Each of these is about the size of a pea. Now back to your scan."

She flicked back and the photo was immediately flooded with golden light with the faint blue outline around the sides. His eyes widened. "It that..."

"Yep," Zachary nodded with a small grin. "The amount of energy you have is so large that it extends beyond your human body."

"But how is that possible?"

"It's not," Loch Ness stated, typing something into the glass frame again and his body lowered back onto the metal table with the lights shutting off.

He rubbed his arm, then hopped off the table and walked over to stand in front of her.

"What does that mean?" he fretted. She turned to him and even though he couldn't see her eyes or her face at all – he felt her gaze boring into him.

Chapter 3

"Nothing to worry about of course," she brushed off casually as Ryder continued to internally scream until his eyes bulged at the pressure in his throat and he forced himself to breathe.

"How –" his voice broke and he coughed, holding up a finger. "How am I not human."

"Well, either your mother has some explaining to do, or you're something that I have never seen before," she said and he had a feeling she was smiling at him.

"Well one of those weird flying wolf eagle things looked at me with a creepy black eye – does that help any?" She tapped the chin of her helmet thoughtfully. "Interesting. Well, I'm staying up all night anyway since it's my shift, so I'll take you to your dorm, then come back.

"Zachary, you are dismissed – make sure you take a look at these scans while I'm gone."

"Gotcha." He grabbed his coat and just as he was halfway through the door, she called

"And Una's teaching you tomorrow night, don't forget." The two of them heard incoherent yells of exasperation from around the corner and Ryder smiled. "I'll show you your room."

He followed her out the door and she closed it behind them, before showing Ryder the other three doors. "The door with the bottle is the medical room as you now know. The dagger is the prototype and testing weapons room. I design armour and weapons, so the newer ones I put in there to be tested. I design them in my room, which is the door with the moon," she pointed to the door and he nodded. "I also make and experiment with new medicines in there. This one is Una's room," she stopped in front of the wooden door with the carved empty circle.

"Why is your room right beside hers?" She turned to him and stared at him silently for a moment.

He had a feeling he'd asked a stupid question.

"I'm her second in command – apart from Meredith and Marcus, I'm the only person she trusts to protect her and stay by her side no matter what."

"So you guys are friends I'm guessing?" he prodded as they walked away towards his room.

"No," she replied. "Merely acquaintances." He laughed.

"Now I'm no expert, but 'acquaintances' usually don't trust each other with their lives. Hm?"

"My Lady doesn't have friends. She's –"

"The leader and everyone is below her, yeah I know – but why can't you guys still be friends?"

"After her mother died with her unborn child, her father died a few years later and Una fell into a downward spiral. She wouldn't eat, drink or go outside. Her powers were out of control. Then her older sibling left and she decided once and for all that she would never rely on anyone ever again.

"Even if she wanted to be my friend, she would force herself not to anyway." Ryder walked in silence for a while. Then an idea popped into his head.

"Can you tell me anything about her siblings?" he asked slowly and carefully – aware he was treading on thin ice.

"I can tell you that her older brother was a coward," she said bluntly. He took a deep breath and kept his eyes on the floor when he asked,

"If her younger sibling was still alive, how old would they be now?"

She stopped abruptly and he slowed to a stop, turning to face her.

"Why the sudden interest in Una's family?" she asked, but her voice held curiosity and no hostility at all. He shrugged, stuffing his hands in his pockets.

"She just seems lonely. I'm interested in what made her like this."

"Nineteen," Loch Ness replied. "They'd be around nineteen years old if they were still alive."

He decided to try his luck.

"Do you know what gender they were?"

"I don't know much, but Lady Nina – Una's mother – wanted another daughter. She decided to keep it a secret, but she seemed exceptionally happy when she found out the gender, so I'm guessing she's female."

His brain whirred for a few moments.

"Is there anything else you can tell me?" She seemed to stare at him for a moment – but she could have been looking at the floor for all he knew.

"Our former Lady wanted to name a child starting with the same letter as her. If the child was still alive, I'm assuming their name would start with an N."

His mind clicked.

"Natalie," he whispered. She cocked her head to the side.

"I'm sorry?"

"Natalie!" he said excitedly, grabbing her hand on instinct and Loch Ness stood there dumbfounded as he jiggled excitedly on the spot. "Think about it – she learns quicker than others, she told me herself, her name starts with an N, she's nineteen and she's even a water elemental. It fits!" She stared at him for a few moments before she spoke.

"Una's brother watched someone run a blade right through Lady Nina's stomach in the midst of battle," she said coldly. "He watched her die. There's no way that her child could have survived."

He went quiet, realised he was still holding her hand – and released it abruptly as if burned by fire.

She continued to walk forward and he trailed after her, his head bowed, but his mind and heart racing as he thought about it.

Natalie was his first suspect and he wasn't going to give up on his idea until he knew for sure that she was just an ordinary water elemental.

They reached his room after a few minutes of deafening silence and when he reached his door, she turned to leave.

"Wait!" she stopped, but didn't turn to face him.

She waited for his response.

"I'm sorry. I crossed the line and I had no right to do that." She turned back around and stepped towards him.

"Lady Una is my best friend, whether she returns my feelings or not. She took me in when no one else wanted me. I've been trying to search for evidence of Nina's unborn child for years now. If there was anything to be found – I would have found it by now." He stood silently in her revelation and waited for her to continue. "I would do anything to give Una her sister back, but I'm afraid she's dead, Ryder. And if my student was that child, I'd know." She put a hand on his shoulder. "Get some sleep. I'll see you next week."

"Loch Ness wait, who saved me from... Well, my world?"

"I did." He blanched slightly.

"I – uh well, um – thanks, I guess."

"You're welcome," she replied, seemingly amused.

"Will you be back when my mum comes here? She'll want to meet the person that saved my life." She shook her head.

"I'm afraid I will still be on my mission," she said softly. "I'll make sure Una will be there to greet her though."

"Okay. Be careful tomorrow," he said out of habit and she nodded.

"I will. Goodnight, Ryder Davis."

"Goodnight," he replied and watched her walk away.

He knew she left as soon as her shift finished in the morning and therefore wasn't expecting to see her until after his mother arrived, but when he woke up in cold sweat with a temperature that hit the roof and fire under his skin, he found out the reason that the academy had an elemental medical specialist.

He'd used the emergency line out of instinct, pressing the button by his bed with the same label as the medical room and within seconds, someone had materialised in the middle of his room and picked him up bridal style with ease.

He vaguely remembered being teleported to the medical room with the person's ice-cold arms around him, soothing his skin – before they set him down on a table and they lost contact completely.

He also remembered crying out for them as his skin burned and feeling their hand on his forehead and comforting words being murmured by his ear.

He was prompted to drink a liquid that tasted like honey and after a few more comforting words, he managed to chew and swallow something that resembled the texture and taste of crushed tea leaves.

His fever subsided and the fire that burned beneath his skin burned out and turned to smouldering ashes that sat at the back of his mind and filled his brain until he couldn't think of anything else than the feeling of sitting across someone's lap with their arms around him, rocking him to sleep like a child.

Then Ryder woke in an unfamiliar bed, with the blanket drawn up to his chin.

He flung back the covers in a panic, putting a hand over his mouth and holding his breath to stop himself from breathing in the toxins.

Then he realised where he was an leaned against the wall with a sigh.

He looked down and by his feet was a vague outline of a human body on the floor in the darkness and after squinting around for a few moments, Ryder realised whoever was on the floor had taken him to their room.

They suddenly exhaled loudly and stretched, squirming onto the other side and blinking sleepily up at him.

"Oh, hey Ryder," Zach said with a lopsided smile. "You feeling okay?" He opened his mouth to respond and let out an embarrassing croak.

The older boy chuckled and sat up, helping Ryder stand and go to the bathroom.

Once the two were dressed, Zachary took Ryder to the medical room for his shift and he sat on one of the medical tables with a blanket draped over his shoulders as Zach worked. Una was scheduled to come and supervise him for his night shift and although it was only morning – Zach was already nervous.

A few people came in before lunch and Ryder was surprised to as how well Zach coped with all his patients. There was a boy who threw up all over the floor and a girl with fourth-degree burns. There was also a boy who had gone completely blind sometime between when he woke up to the end of training. One girl was even crying blood and had an atrocious nosebleed – to which Zach had to call Loch Ness to consult in her.

"Blood coming from the eyes and nose," he said once she answered. "Nowhere else, no." he checked inside her mouth while humming in response whatever the girl was saying on the other end of the line.

"Earth elemental. Yeah, it's really sticky." He frowned. "Oh? Okay, I'll check." He took a sample of the blood and scanned it, to which he nodded and answered, "Yeah, it is." He listened for a few seconds. "Top shelf? Okay, got it." He ended the call and threw something at Ryder with a quick, "—catch."

He almost had a heart attack and fumbled, but managed to catch it eventually.

It was a smooth, polished ball of silver around the size and shape of a flat river pebble.

"The key to Loch Ness's room," he said when Ryder gave him a baffled look. "I need to get something but –" The girl suddenly lurched forward and spat out a huge blob of red onto Zach's shirt and he gave Ryder a pleading look.

He slid off the desk and nodded. "Okay, what do you need."

"She has shelves all around her room – check the top of every one of them until you find a vial of green liquid."

"Alright," he walked out of the medical room – leaning heavily on the wall for support – and stood in front of her door. The carving of a moon sat at around eye-level, with a groove winding down from the moon to the lock like a river with smooth bends.

Except where a lock usually was on these doors was a square piece of metal.

He frowned at it for a few seconds, then looked at the piece in his hand and pressed the two together.

They connected with a small metallic click and nothing happened.

He looked around, checking whether anyone saw, then sighed in relief when there wasn't.

He then began to feel around the sides of the square and when he got to the bottom side, it flicked up, revealing a tiny hole.

Feeling ridiculous, he attempted to fit the large piece of metal into the pea-sized hole and found it simply slid right in – changing shape to fit it while staying completely solid.

The metal pebble was sucked out of his hand and he saw that a trail of silver began winding up the groove on the door towards the carving – then filled it with metallic silver, and making the moon glow.

The door slid open with a click and he smiled to himself. "Nice," he commented, walking inside.

The moment he did so, fires lit on both sides and he let out a small surprised yelp, backing up against the closed door.

He caught his breath and sighed, eyes flicking around the room.

The room was perfectly circular in shape, but the walls weren't walls at all – they were shelves.

Right across from him were two doors – one was painted black with sparkling stars and the other had winding plants with blooming black flowers. They both sat in the middle of the wall, with the shelves all around them.

Right in the middle of the room, was a bed set into the floor – like a small den below the wooden floorboards – and a wooden table hovered directly above the bed. Just like the metal scanners in the medical room, it also didn't have any legs, but this one was filled with books, writing materials, small weapons and even a helmet that looked exactly like the one Loch Ness wore.

He shrugged and turned to the shelves, checking the top one of each for a green liquid, but couldn't find anything even remotely green.

He sighed and turned to leave, but stopped, turning back to look at the two doors opposite him, with a fire torch between them.

He pushed the starry one open and fire torches lit automatically.

He gaped with wide eyes at the room.

It was around the size of the main room and was also circular in shape, with a ledge sticking out around the wall as a table.

Shelves were filled with weapons and armour of every kind and ones that he'd never seen before.

A microscope sat in the corner, pointed down at a small circle of metal. An axe sat on the table around the room, with various other weapons strewn across the tables. A few skin-tight suits in various colours were hung on the walls and two spiked helmets sat on the shelves.

What made him stop in his tracks however, was the cylindrical glass case in the middle of the room.

Suspended in the air inside it was what looked like a black, one-piece swimsuit.

It glittered when he moved his head from side to side and spread from the back was a pair of massive metal wings. Yet another spiked helmet hovered above the main piece and a pair of leather combat boots sat at the bottom of the tank. Hanging above the boots were black pants with grey knitted leg warmers from the ankles to below the knees. A matching black jacket with a silver zip and trim by the pockets completed the set.

He stood dumbfounded for a moment before jumping in fear when someone knocked on the door.

"Ryder? You okay in there?"

"Y-yeah!" he called, rushing out and closing the door behind him, his heart thumping in his chest.

"Did you find – oh damn she – just hurry up would you?" His voice came from beyond the front door and Ryder heard thundering footsteps rush back to the medical room.

He quickly opened the door to the next room and saw bubbling cauldrons, plants in bottles and growing out of the floor, and even a large glass tank with a raging red liquid in it that slammed against the glass and shrieked at him.

He quickly slammed the door shut and stumbled to the front door in a daze.

It was only then that he realised there were shelves above the main door too, and right on the top one rested a small bottle of green liquid.

He grinned and quickly grabbed the chair by the bed right in the middle of the room and dragged it over to reach the bottle, clambered down and rushed back to the medical room.

The girl was sitting upright with her knees to her chest and sobbing as blood ran from her ears.

Ryder stood frozen in the door with wide eyes and Zachary ran over and snatched the bottle, bringing it over and forcing the girl to lie down and drip the liquid in her eyes.

After a while, she stopped crying and when Zach wiped the blood from her nose, it wasn't immediately replaced with fresh streams of red.

She thanked the two of them and while Zach talked to a young boy who had come in, Ryder helped the girl lie down on one of the beds and she fell asleep within seconds, energy wasted.

He sat down on the one he was perched on before and sat silently with his legs dangling off the edge.

"Hey, Ryder. It's lunchtime – which is break time for us." He looked up and nodded, still in a daze, and wandered over to him with the blanket over his shoulders, dragging on the floor.

Zachary suddenly took hold of his shoulders and stopped him from moving through the doorway, glaring into his eyes.

"Are you okay? How do you feel? Hot?" he put a hand on his forehead and Ryder smirked, swaying on his feet.

"I'm always hot," he slurred.

"Okay no. You're not going anywhere," Zach instructed.

"But it's lunchtime," he whined childishly as his vision started blurring, Zach's face going in and out of focus.

He felt himself being carried to another room and placed on the bed.

"It's hot," he cried, flinging the blankets off.

Zach put a hand on his arm to stop him and leapt back, wringing his hand with a hiss.

"You were fine four seconds ago," he panicked, running a hand through his hair.

Ryder began taking his shirt off and Zach didn't stop him.

"I'll be back, don't move." And he ran out, one hand on his earpiece.

Without a shirt was better, but Ryder was still burning up.

He stumbled into the bathroom and filled the tub with cold water and without even taking his trousers off – dove right in and lay at the bottom of the tub, waiting for it to fill up.

Once it was half full, he took a deep breath in and put his head underwater.

It stole the heat from his forehead and cheeks and he closed his eyes, letting the air bubbles escape from between his lips.

Then he was yanked out of bliss.

"Are you trying to drown yourself!?" Zach hissed, dragging him out and wrapping a towel around his shoulders.

He put a thermometer in the water that was now steaming and his eyes widened.

"That's almost boiling – what do I do!?" he rambled.

"Call Una," came a familiar voice from the metal box on his hip.

"Loch Ness?" Ryder asked, his eyes wide in surprise.

"Ryder listen to me – I'm currently in a place where I can't teleport back to you and it will take me at least seven hours to get to the nearest place where I can. Zachary will take care of you. Listen to everything he says, okay?"

"But –"

"You heard her," Zachary snapped.

"Try to keep his temperature down until Una gets there. Focus on keeping him in one spot – I'll call her." There was a click and several seconds later, their leader materialised in the middle of the room.

She walked over and took her armour off, then shrugged off her jacket and began unbuttoning her shirt.

"My Lady –" Zachary said, but she ignored him and yanked Ryder into her lap.

She wrapped her arms around him and Ryder leaned into her touch.

Her skin was ice-cold.

She focused and ice crystals began forming on Ryder's skin, and as the girl swiped her hand over his forehead, his sweat froze and he sighed in relief.

Zachary visibly relaxed.

"Thanks," Ryder gasped weakly and she gave him a smile.

He would have marvelled at the rarity of it, but he was already slipping into unconsciousness.

When he woke, he was no longer covered in ice and was lying on one of the hospital beds.

The girl from before was sitting cross-legged on the edge of the bed with a bright smile.

"Hey, how are you feeling?" she asked and he groaned.

"Terrible. How are you feeling? Last time I saw you, you were crying blood."

"Much better now, but it was tree sap actually, not blood. Since I'm an Earth elemental and the substance was really sticky, Loch Ness deduced it wasn't blood and was able to treat me." He looked at her with wide eyes.

"O-o-o-kay... anyway, would you mind helping me up? My whole body is made of jelly right now."

She nodded and helped him sit up and he leaned heavily on her side.

"What's your name?" he asked and she shifted below his head, dropping her shoulder so he could lean on her more comfortably.

"Naomi," she said softly.

"That's a nice name," he commented. "I'm Ryder." She chuckled.

"I know. I've heard about you from Loch Ness." He perked up instantly.

"She talks about me?"

"I mean, she did. She was sent on a mission to your world just to take samples and make a report to Una, but instead, she brought back you."

"You two are... close?" She shifted on the table with a smile.

"Well, I'm one of her main students – she teaches me close-combat privately, and she doesn't do that for anyone else, so I guess you can say we're close." He suddenly took his head off her shoulder and looked up at her.

"Would you say you learn faster than others?" She frowned at the ground.

"Well, I guess so. Loch Ness wouldn't have taken me up as a student if I didn't. You know it's kind of strange – she only teaches people who are really powerful and learn quickly. I mean – I get she's the best teacher out there shy of Una and Meredith and Marcus, but she still doesn't take up... normal students, you know?"

She's only taking up Nina's potential children as students, to keep tabs on them,

Ryder realised.

He tried to ask as nonchalantly as possible, "Would you say you and Una are close?" She barked out a laugh.

"Not a chance. That girl's terrifying."

Ryder smiled at her but mentally added Naomi to his list of potential royals.

She talked with him for a few more minutes until Zachary came back – and learned that she was Loch Ness's best physical combat student, that one of her grandparents were Chinese and the rest of her family was European, and that Loch Ness was currently on a mission to map a section of the realm that had a dark history and had a tendency to kill anyone who went remotely near it.

Which had him worrying about her safety for the rest of the day.

Being sick did have its perks actually – which Ryder found when he had an excuse to stay in the library and sneak around while everyone was training.

To his surprise, Naomi actually helped him find whatever he was looking for.

And once he had a good collection of books sitting in front of him on the table, she finally turned to him and asked, "So... what's all this for?" He flicked the first book open – the history of all the Kediotherylan realm's leaders – and pondered telling her.

"I'm researching your history," he said blankly, flicking to the last few pages and seeing a family portrait popping up.

"Oh, okay." He stared at the coloured picture of a beautiful, well-muscled Chinese woman standing beside a tall English man with a sword in the floor between them. They both had a hand on the hilt, the man's hand wrapping around the woman's smaller one.

In her other arm, the woman held a baby wrapped in golden silk – that stared up at her mother with gleaming brown eyes.

Standing between the two parents was a young boy in a navy blue jacket and black pants, clutching onto the edge of his father's armour with his mouth open as if he was saying something when the picture was taken. He had black hair that came down to the middle of his neck and rosy cheeks.

"Is that..." he pointed to the girl and Naomi nodded.

"Lady Una," she said with a smile. "According to my mum, she was the cutest thing ever." His head snapped up.

"Your mum?"

"I'm adopted," she said, looking down at the picture. "I don't know who my real parents are. It's really strange – when I did a DNA test, they could find my parents' and grandparents' nationalities – but not who they were. It's like they were completely deleted from the system – but only specific parts." She lay her head on her arms and sighed. "They probably went against the law and were exiled to the human realm. When that happens, they're always deleted from the system so they can no longer re-enter our society."

He nodded silently, brain whizzing in so many different directions he couldn't focus on the book in front of him for a few seconds.

Then he shook his head and flicked to the next page.

"How can you print so many books? Won't the trees run out?" She grinned at him, wiggling her wingers.

"Earth elementals," she said and his mouth made an o shape.

"Right. But you can't grow trees yourself?"

"Yep," she put her feet up on the chair opposite her, crossing her ankles below the table. "We have to get a water elemental to help us. It's basically our conjoined power." He nodded and his eyes landed on a picture of Lady Nina standing in front of a gnarled tree with drooping branches, with one hand on the small of her back and another on her swollen belly.

Written underneath in small words was – taken a month before Lady Nina and her child were killed in a battle November the 20th, 2472.

A picture was in the middle of the page to the left, of a woman dressed in army green with overlapping black and green armour and a mask depicting the snarling face of a wolf. The caption read – The famous Earth elemental Alpha, the leader of the rebellion.

According to the book, it was she who had killed Nina.

He flicked through the pages and found information on Una, but skipped it – not particularly wanting to read about the tragic past he already knew.

The pages on her brother had been ripped out by the spine and tear marks dotted the next page, making the black text run and blur.

He swallowed roughly and slammed the book shut, scaring Naomi.

"You okay?" she asked worriedly and he nodded sharply.

He didn't need to ask who had ripped the pages out.

"Are you part of a team?" he asked instead. She nodded.

"The senior teams are always well balanced – some are good with speed, others with strength, some with combat and others with their elements. Junior teams like mine, however, have members with similar strengths – so all of us are strong in close-combat."

"Are there any other humans here?"

"I only know one other apart from you," she said, staring into the distance with her eyes glazed over.

But I'm not human.

She licked her lips and frowned. "His name's Ainsley, I think."

"How old is he?" He flicked open another book – one on all the battles that happened in the Kediotherylan realm and browsed it for 'battles for Earth.' He looked up and saw Naomi giving him the raised eyebrow look his father usually gave him. "Huh? What?"

"I said, he's eighteen. Acts like a fucking child," she said heatedly. He gave her the raised eyebrow look back. "He knows he won't get exiled, so he thinks he can do whatever he wants. Every time that Una has wanted to kick him out, Loch Ness talks her out of it. The most irritating thing is, he knows how far he can go, so all Loch Ness has to do is point out he hasn't gone against any laws and Una can't do anything about it." She suddenly leaned in, eyes flicking around the room. "You know," she whispered. "She believes that Nina's youngest child is still alive. She's asked me to help her find information for her before." His eyes widened.

"Really?" She nodded with a hum. "Asked you to help her?" Naomi looked a little offended. "Oh no I just realised how that sounded – that's not what I meant," he blabbed. She smirked.

"And what did you mean?" she prompted.

He hastily returned to reading, almost climbing right into the pages in embarrassment.

She grinned, leaning back in her chair and watching him slowly lower the book when his flushed cheeks began to subside. "I can introduce you to Ainsley later if you want," Naomi offered, checking her watch. "It's five o clock now, dinner's in an hour so I can introduce you then."

"The dining hall's massive though, how will you find him?" She gave him a weary look.

"Trust me on this one." He frowned, but nodded, going back to reading through the books silently until they left for dinner.

Chapter 4

"Oh," Ryder said stupidly as he stood in front of a massive food war going on in the corner of the dining hall. "That, would be me."

"Yeah," she elbowed him in the side. "Come on." He followed her over and right in the middle of the war was a boy in the blood red coloured fire elemental robes, wrestling with someone wearing a black leather jacket.

Naomi stood silently until the elemental noticed her – and he only did so one he had grabbed a fistful of the other boy's hair and was getting ready to whack him with a chicken drumstick.

She raised an eyebrow and the other boy finally turned his head, sheepishly grinning up at her even though his hair was still in the elemental's grasp. "Hey! Naomi! Uh... how have you been?"

"Fine," she growled heatedly. She jerked her head to the side roughly and the fire elemental clambered off him, returning to his meal like nothing had ever happened.

"So, what brings you here? To see me, I mean? I bet you're not here to see Caleb – downright asshole, he –" a chicken drumstick hit him in the side of the face. He roared and launched himself at the snickering fire elemental, but the table suddenly changed shape – coiling out towards him and grabbing him around the waist and lowering him to the ground – screaming and kicking – so he never even touched the boy.

Ryder gave Naomi and awed look and she quickly averted her eyes and he was surprised to see she went a little pink.

"I'll fucking get you one day," he yelled at the boy, pointing menacingly.

"Sure," he snickered back and the boy waved a fist at him angrily.

"Children, children," Naomi sighed and the boy gave her a look so offended that Ryder otherwise would have guessed she's insulted his fashion sense. "Anyway I'm not here to stay – I've brought you a friend." She nudged Ryder in the shoulder – hard – and he tumbled towards the boy.

"What? I don't even know him!" They both cried in unison.

"Ainsley – Ryder. Ryder – Ainsley." She then smiled and walked away, calling over her shoulder: "Ask Una where I am if you need me!"

"Jerk," the boy whined and Ryder couldn't help but chuckle, stuffing his hands in his pockets. The boy grinned. "So, Ryder, what are you?"

"Uh... Human??" he muttered, still unsure what he really was and the boy's eyes lit up.

"Oh, you're Ryder! Like – Ryder, Ryder. The Ryder. Right?"

"That's me?" he said with a shrug and the boy pumped his fist in the air with an excited whoop.

"Man, we are going to have so much fun – what's your room number?"

"Two five nine – no idea where that is though."

"No way – I'm two five three! How come I never saw you?" He shrugged.

"I've been here and there lately – spent most of the time in the elemental medical room with Naomi."

"What? Why?" his eyes widened. "Oh my god did you get her pregnant?"

"What!? No! I barely know her!!" He sighed in relief.

"Oh thank god – sorry, it's just they never send humans in there unless they're related to the reason an elemental needs to be there." He suddenly frowned at him suspiciously. "Why were you there then?"

"I had a fever and I didn't know where the human medical room was, so I just wandered in and Zachary treated me." It wasn't a lie – just missing some very important truths.

Ainsley shrugged.

"Fair enough. Hey, have you tried the apple crumble here? It's to die for." Ryder shook his head and the boy gasped dramatically, hopping up and yelling something about getting him some.

Maybe he's not so bad, Ryder thought.

He met his father just before he went back to his room, assuring him that he'd be fine – Ainsley was taking him back to his dorm –

and promised to spend some dad and son time with him before his mother arrived. Scott stopped him before he left and told him that the next day he had prepared to have Ryder sit in one of his elemental classes.

As Ryder walked back to Ainsley's room, he asked – "What did you do that made Naomi despise you so much?"

"You mean like the last thing I did, or in general?" Ryder gave him a sceptical look. "Oh okay, fine. She didn't like me the moment I was brought here by Celine. Saved me from your world too – I was about to be... reaped."

"Ten billion or less," Ryder muttered and Ainsley nodded.

"That's right. I was six years old – she simply scooped me up and teleported straight out of there. Teams aren't meant to get involved, which is why she got in trouble with Una's advisors. She was almost exiled."

"What's that got to do with anything?" Ryder asked and Ainsley gave him a grim smile.

"Celine is Naomi's adoptive mother."

"Oh." Ainsley sighed.

"Yeah. If she had been exiled – Naomi would have been left with no one. So in a way, it was kind of my fault. I didn't use to understand why she despised me so much – she was just that seven-year-old kid that glared at me from the other end of the room as I clung to her mother, terrified of her." He chuckled slightly. "And as I grew up I started playing pranks on her. Tricks. Tried to side up with Celine as much as I could just to piss her off. And I guess it worked.

"After I found out why she hated me so much – I felt really bad for all the things I'd done. But I was a coward and I still am. I don't have the guts to apologise. I guess I'm kind of scared she won't forgive me." There was a moment of silence and Ryder gave him a tentative smile.

"So... What was the latest thing you did?" He gave Ryder a more genuine smile.

"Well you see, she's fuckin' terrified of snakes right, so I get this rubber one and put it on her bed – I have access to her room because of Celine – and like an hour later she comes running out of her room screeching like a pterodactyl, scared shitless. You honestly should have seen her face." Ryder shook his head with a chuckle.

"Does she get back at you?" He scoffed with wide eyes.

"Oh yeah."

"Care to share?"

"Hell no – go ask her," he shoved Ryder playfully and he gasped, shoving him back.

Ainsley then took to shoving him straight into the wall and dashing off down the hallway.

"Unfair!!" Ryder yelled after him.

He was a good four metres behind, and Ainsley obviously trained because Ryder almost immediately began to fall behind.

He was about to get to the door and it was clear his intention was to lock Ryder out – so with a final burst of speed, he thrust his palm out and yelled, "STOP!"

A wall of crackling and snapping fire burst straight out of the floor and rose up like a demon out of hell from the floor beneath Ainsley's feet.

He swore whole-heartedly and skidded to a stop right before he tumbled into the raging inferno, then it snapped out like a light and he slowly turned around to give Ryder the most horrified look he'd ever seen.

He looked at his hand.

Then he looked at Ainsley.

"What the actual fuck was that," the boy whispered, for once keeping his voice low.

"I have no idea," Ryder panicked in a low voice back and Ainsley slowly walked over, pointing a finger at him.

"Was that you?"

"I-I don't know man it just..."

"Boom," Ainsley shook his head. "Mate I don't know what's wrong with you, but whatever it is, we have to tell someone about it. Let's contact –"

"Loch Ness."

"—Zachary." He squinted at Ryder. "What? Why? She won't be back for like another..." he counted on his fingers with a confused frown. "I don't know – six days??"

"We can still contact her, she is the elemental specialist after all."

"Yes but Zachary's her apprentice, he knows what to do."

"I don't think so," Ryder muttered, but the boy heard.

"Oh alright fine – we'll contact Una, who can hopefully get in contact with her. But first – we need to scope the area for fire elementals."

"Why?" Ryder asked, bewildered. Ainsley squinted around the hallway.

"Because I bet you twenty that Caleb's around the corner laughing his smug little ass off."

"Twenty what?" Ryder was even more baffled.

"I – you... You know what, forget it. It's a currency in another parallel universe."

"Another one?"

"Yeah, there aren't only two in the whole universe you know. There are way, way more – most of which we're pretty much banned from visiting. Then there was that whole alien race that tried to use us as pets – wait we're meant to be looking for Caleb! He's probably gone by now!"

"Ainsley wait – would Caleb really do that?" he asked seriously and the boy shrugged pathetically.

"Gee man, I don't know, but he's never done something like this before. He doesn't usually use his elemental powers against me – despite being an ass he does make the fight fair since I'm human."

"Okay," Ryder sighed. "So it was possibly me right?"

"Or there's another fire elemental out to get me," Ainsley said, going back to squinting suspiciously around the hallway. Ryder groaned and grabbed him by the arm to stop him, but Ainsley shrieked and leapt back.

"Shit man, your arm's burning hot!" he wrung his hand and when he stopped, Ryder saw that his skin was red.

"This happened before," he said, with his eyes wide.

"What!?"

"Come on we have to go see Zachary now, he can contact Una." Ainsley for once didn't argue and the two ran all the way to the medical room.

By the time they got there and the door opened, Ryder was so light-headed he simply fell right through the doorway and landed on Zachary.

He hissed in pain and dragged Ryder over to the table, before wringing his hands and checking his shoulder for burns.

As suspected, he immediately called Una, but Ryder stopped her before she was able to do anything.

"Wait, I don't feel hot this time," he muttered, swaying unsteadily.

Zachary made him lie down, muttering something about Loch Ness having his liver for breakfast if Ryder hurt himself.

"Well, you most certainly are," Una said, to which he considered joking around with her, but even his disorientated brain knew not to mess with the Queen of the Kediotherylan realm, so he shut up.

"He's actually not as hot as he was last time, but you should still... do whatever you did last time," Zachary muttered, moving to call Loch Ness.

Seeing as Ryder wasn't screaming in pain this time, Una simply took his hand and let the ice crystals wander up his arm.

"Wicked," Ainsley whispered and Una glared in his direction.

He shut up immediately and Ryder almost laughed.

"So how do you feel?" Zach asked, still trying to call Loch Ness.

"Don't bother," Una said after he tried to call her the fourth time. "She's gone into the Dead Zone."

"Dead Zone!?" Ryder shrieked.

"Okay just calm down –" Zach said, trying to push him back down onto the bed.

"Ryder, you will lie down, you will rest and you will let Zachary examine you and answer all his medical questions and that is a direct order," Una hissed.

Ryder stopped struggling and found himself lying down against his will. He didn't fight it – because he wanted to lie down, he wanted to rest. "That's better," Una said with a small smile. He felt a strange sense of calm wash over him.

"How did you do that?" he slurred, blinking sleepily.

"All elementals feel a connection to me that they can't ignore. I can hide it, or I can use it to control my subjects." She didn't seem to want to continue talking about the subject, because she put a hand on Zachary's shoulder, whispered something, then walked into a closed-off room by the end of the medical room and Ryder vaguely remembered that she was meant to help him with something that night... Something to do with Loch Ness??

"Okay, how do you feel?"

"I feel normal, but I have a headache."

"Anything else?"

"I feel dizzy... and tired. Weak."

"Okay, how bad is the headache from one to ten?"

"Ten being...?" Zachary smiled slightly.

"Being stabbed in the skull."

"Like a six," he groaned. "Can Una help?"

"It doesn't work that way, I'm afraid. She can only make you feel certain emotions and make you do things – she can't trick your brain into thinking something doesn't hurt."

"That's weirdly specific," Ryder grumbled.

"Mhm." He jabbed something into Ryder's arm.

"Ow," he said dully, glaring with all the force he could muster.

"Sorry," Zachary grinned, not looking very sorry at all.

Naomi burst through the door at full force and Zachary screamed.

"How is he!?" she panted, rushing over.

"I'm fine," Ryder said heatedly and she took his face in her hands, turning his head from side to side and putting a hand on his forehead.

"You have a temperature," she said worriedly and Zachary snorted.

"No, really? You should have come here earlier – we couldn't even touch him."

"Why, was he that hot?" Naomi asked.

Ryder smirked and opened his mouth.

"You, shut up," Zachary hissed and he pouted, but closed his mouth again.

"You should be fine if you just sleep – I'm up all night for my shift anyway so I'll check up on you. Una can help, she's supervising me."

"I'll keep an eye on him," Naomi volunteered, immediately plopping down on the seat by his bed.

"You can't stay up all night – you have training with Loch Ness's group tomorrow."

"They won't miss me," she said dismissively.

"It's fine, you can go, I'm sure Una's capable of taking care of me," Ryder said quietly.

"I'm staying," she said firmly and that was that.

Ryder noticed that Zachary left his side a few minutes later to tend to someone who had just walked in and before he slipped into unconsciousness, he felt Naomi's hand slip into his and hold it gently.

"I'm not leaving," she said quietly, as if he needed reminding. "It's my duty to protect you."

"Why?" he whispered, on the verge of sleep, his mind muddled. What is she doing?

"It's my duty to keep everyone safe," she said so quietly he wasn't sure whether he'd imagined it or not, then he tipped off the edge into the abyss of sleep.

When he woke, it was quite obviously either very late into the night or very early in the morning, as there were several people now lying in small soundproof capsules around the hospital beds.

What had woken him, however, was the feeling of Naomi's hand being pulled from his own.

He looked up and saw Una leaning over the girl as she lifted her up bridal style and smiled down at her, unaware Ryder had woken.

She placed the sleeping girl on the bed beside Ryder, activated a soundproof bubble and then walked over and sat beside him where Naomi sat just moments before.

He tried to go back to sleep, but sneezed loudly – showing he was awake.

Una didn't seem surprised. "You feeling better?" she asked, still watching the earth elemental as her chest rose and fell with each breath.

"Yeah," he sat up, surprising himself when he didn't feel like throwing up.

"I'm sorry I woke you," she said quietly, finally turning to him.

Her eyes were icy blue and glowed in the darkness.

"It's fine – I probably would have woken up soon anyway." He moved his head from side to side and winced at the symphony of cracks and pops. "I've been doing a lot of sleeping lately."

"Loch Ness was much like you when she first got her element." He chuckled.

"Turning into a bonfire in the middle of the night?" She shook her head.

"No, she turned to ice." His eyes widened.

"Literally or figuratively?"

"Both. A bit like you – she looked fine, but when I touched her skin, ice crystals formed on my fingers. Water elementals usually have bouts of cold sweat and frigid skin, the opposite of fire elementals."

"What about earth and air elementals then?"

"Earth elementals have excruciating pains – like their bones are growing too big for their body." Ryder winced. "Air elementals are the luckiest of us all – they simply pass out for a few days, then wake up with no memory they had ever fallen over in the middle of training two days ago."

"Really?" Ryder laughed. She hummed in response with a smile.

"A little inconvenient when they get older – one of the air elementals on Loch Ness's team simply dropped in the middle of a battle. Almost got killed and it's quite unlucky he didn't because Loch Ness almost skinned him alive once he woke. She took a bullet for him, that girl – I admire her strength."

"So... How long did it take for Loch Ness to recover?"

"Not long at all. She sat up all night most days working on a cure so she could get back on her feet and tend to her patients." Her eyes dimmed slightly and Ryder was shocked that her irises actually dulled their natural glow. "And I could do nothing to help her."

"Why?"

"My power is ice. Anything I did would only hurt her more. So Veronica sat with her night after night, curled up beside her to keep her warm while she worked."

"Veronica?"

"Loch Ness's fire elemental. They were just friends before, but when Loch Ness was ready to pick a team she plucked Veronica straight out of the bunch of seniors with such speed I could have sworn she just teleported that poor girl right over to her." She chuckled softly with a small, sad smile. "That's why I want to help you. Because... Maybe all that time I spent sitting by Loch Ness – useless – I might be able to make up by helping ease your pain instead."

His eyes flicked up to her and she smiled.

"Get some rest. You should be tired – at this stage it's normal." He yawned.

"I'm not... tired," he said moodily and she chuckled and he felt her fingers brush the hair out of his face.

"Of course you're not," she whispered and her voice drifted away along with the rest of the world as he fell asleep.

This time he woke to see Naomi by his side on the chair Una was on before – holding his hand.

He shifted to sit up, trying not to wake her, but the moment he moved his hand, her head jerked up with wild eyes and her hair sticking up in several odd places. "Oh, hey!" she said quickly, dragging her fingers through her hair. "How are you feeling?"

"Somehow, I get asked that a lot now," he said with a frown.

"Well, you need to be taken care of, you're helpless on your own," she said with a grin.

"I take offence to that," he scowled, swinging his legs over the side of the bed.

"Whoa whoa whoa, where do you think you're going?"

"I need to pee," he said huffily. "Unless of course, you want to watch me."

"Uh, no need," she muttered and he grinned.

"Good. Then stay here and get some sleep."

"Why?"

"Don't think I didn't notice you crawled straight back once you realised Una had taken you to another bed."

"I'll be waiting here," she responded, avoiding his statement.

He managed to stumble to the bathroom and back again without bumping into anything and the moment he got back he revealed to Naomi he was going back to the library.

To which she said – to put it delicately – that he was an idiot.

"You're in no state to be wandering around the place!" she'd said.

But there they were, with Ryder smugly waggling his eyebrows at her over the spine of his book and he could have sworn her cheeks went pink, but then she lifted her book up over her face so he couldn't see her.

Ainsley wandered into the library about an hour later and grinned at him. "Zachary said you might be here."

"Zachary? How did he know that?" Ainsley shrugged.

"Ask him." Then he saw Naomi and scowled.

She glared right back.

"Asshole," she grunted.

"Nippity snippet," he blabbed back.

"That's not a word," she snapped.

"That's because it's two words," he said, sliding down into the seat next to Ryder to which she glared at him harder from across the table.

"Describe 'Nippity Snippet,'" she said, crossing her arms and leaning her elbows on the book in front of her.

"In two words?" he taunted and she leaned forward.

"Yeah." He leaned closer too so their noses were almost touching.

"Naomi Howell."

She narrowed her eyes and the wood of the table wrapped around his throat and his eyes went wide.

Ryder's eyes snapped to her with a horrified, "Naomi!" and she released him immediately, almost embarrassed.

Ainsley rubbed his neck with a scowl. "Nippity Snippit," he hissed.

"Asshole," she retorted.

"Children, children," Ryder quoted her and Ainsley snickered.

"See, he's on my side now," he stated smugly.

Naomi threw her chair back and looked ready to murder him, but then someone said Ryder's name and the three of them turned – the earth elemental's arm raised with a book in her hand that was about to be swept in a wide arc towards Ainsley's nose and he was just about halfway under the table.

Ryder had one hand in her direction and the other in front of Ainsley as if that alone would stop the book from decapitating him.

"Oh uh, hi Natalie!" he said with a slightly scared smile, but Naomi lowered the book and he visibly exhaled.

"Nat!" the girl walked over and embraced the other girl in a hug. The two were actually visibly similar, except Naomi was slightly shorter and had a softer face, while Natalie's was more angular like Una's.

"Birds of same feather flock together," Ainsley said from his side.

"Until the cat comes," Ryder finished and Ainsley's eyebrows furrowed.

"Wait is that the end of the –"

"You know Naomi? I thought you didn't know anyone," Natalie interrupted with a smile.

"I met her yesterday, long story. Anyway, no offence but what are you doing here? Aren't you Loch Ness's substitute?"

"Yeah, but," she said with a smile. "Her team wants to meet you."

"Meet me?" Ryder asked with wide eyes.

"Yep," Natalie nodded and both Naomi and Ainsley looked like their favourite toy had just been stolen from right underneath their noses.

"I need to ask Marina something, I'll walk with you?" Naomi asked Natalie. The girl shrugged.

"Sure."

"I need to talk to James," Ainsley blurted. "So I can take Ryder there if you want?" Naomi glared.

"How about we all just walk together?" Natalie asked, seemingly baffled about the whole ordeal.

Ryder wasn't exactly sure what was going on either and eyed the two that were facing off silently in a language of glares and eyebrow raises.

"Fine," the two said at the same time, straightened and stood on either side of Ryder.

Natalie seemed even more baffled than before, but led the way.

They reached the training room – which Ryder hadn't ever visited before – and when Natalie pushed the doors open his eyebrows just about disappeared into his hairline.

About the size of ten football fields, it had a roof that disappeared into the distance with twinkling lights on the ceiling and hundreds of students training on various equipment.

"They're at the sparring circles," Natalie said, wandering forward.

"Pick your jaw off the ground," Natalie giggled, using her hand to push his jaw up and he closed his mouth.

They reached a circle that was around five metres in diameter and which had two people sparring in it.

They were throwing punches and kicks and calculated flips that forced each other back towards the edges of the circle.

There was suddenly a blast of fire and Ryder leapt back into Naomi, who thankfully managed to catch him without falling over.

The stream of flame stope halfway to the second figure, who pushed his palms forward and forced it back with a blast of air that fuelled the fire and shoved it right into the woman's face with twice the power she threw it at him with.

It didn't affect her as it was her own magic, but the flames distracted her for a second which was all the man needed to take her legs out from under her and roll on top of her with his fist by her nose.

"I win," he panted and she shrugged him off her stomach with a scowl.

"Again."

"Hey, I brought Ryder over," Natalie said, but her voice was quiet, as if she were speaking to people her senior – who were above her in ranking.

Which was strange because she was meant to be leading the group.

"Hey Naomi!" A short blonde woman with the same army green robes as Naomi wandered over and hugged the girl.

"Ryder, this is Marina," Naomi introduced with a smile.

She turned to him and looked up into his brown eyes with baby blue ones that glittered.

"Pleasure to meet you," she said curtly, shaking his hand.

"T-the pleasure is mine," managed to force out and she quickly ushered him over to the sparring ring.

The woman in blood red robes was dusting herself off, flicking her dirty blonde hair out of her face. "Hello," she said, holding out her hand. "I'm –"

"Veronica," Ryder interrupted, shaking her hand warmly with a grin. She raised an eyebrow. "Una talked about you," he said and the man beside her elbowed her in the ribs – waggling his eyebrows.

She punched him in the shoulder.

"Ow! I didn't even say anything!"

"You thought it though," she growled, her cheeks tinged with pink. "Don't worry about it, he's an idiot," she reassured Ryder.

"I'm Sam," the man introduced. "Heard you've become acquainted with Ainsley."

"That's right," he said slowly.

"Acts like a kid," he shook his head. "Sometimes it's hard to believe he's only two years younger than me."

"You're twenty?"

"Yeah."

"No way – how could you do all that..." Ryder waved his hands around in front of his face.

"Training," Veronica quipped. "Anyway, we wanted you here to meet the team – Loch Ness wanted you to meet us anyway. You've met our earth and air elemental already and I'm our firepower. Loch Ness is our water elemental and James is our second air elemental. Absolute knucklehead."

Ainsley gasped from behind Ryder.

"How dare you, James is an absolute babe."

"A what?" Ryder asked, baffled.

"Ainsley spends too much in the... other dimension." Veronica said.

"Other dimension??"

"How about we go see James," Marina said quickly.

"I already told him we're in an alternate dimension," Ainsley shrugged. "I think Loch Ness told him first."

Ryder was completely overwhelmed by everyone talking at once and Marina was obviously the only one who noticed. "I said let's go see James," she instructed and Veronica rolled her eyes.

"He's not here."

"What? He's meant to be –"

"Training Michael, yeah I know. He stormed off in a rage last time I saw him, I don't know what Mike did this time." Ryder almost yanked his hair out in frustration.

"Who's Michael –"

Chapter 5

Ryder whipped around to see a boy that looked like he was in his mid-teens, with a mass of curly red on the top of his head and green eyes that looked like they were permanently filled to the brim with m i s - chief.

"Little Michael Macintosh," Sam said, bringing him into a choke-hold and ruffling up his hair roughly until the boy screamed.

He threw himself away from the man with a scowl, flattening down his hair and straightening out his shirt.

The man chuckled and flicked his sweaty black hair away from his forehead.

"What did you do to James?" Marina asked, getting straight to the point with her hands on her hips.

"Nothing," he said with a frown, completely innocent and even slightly confused.

"Don't use that voice on me," she warned, waggling a finger at him. The boy grinned suddenly.

"You couldn't even tell I was lying could you." She growled at him and he laughed.

"Loch Ness has this uncanny way of telling whether he's lying or not," Sam said with a shake of his head. "I don't know how she does it – he's a right little devil."

"I just told him if his ears were any bigger they could be a radio dish," he said simply with a shrug.

"Michael," Marina scolded.

"But it's true," he exclaimed, putting a hand on his heart. "And Loch Ness taught me never to lie."

"Lord give me the strength to get through this day," Veronica hissed, cuffing the boy around the ear. He yelped and glared up at her and she threw him a withering glare back.

"Well since James isn't here, don't you have somewhere to be?" Naomi said a little too cheerfully.

Ainsley glared.

"Not really. I have a lot of spare time on my hands – and don't you need to talk to Marina?"

"I just did," she sassed back, crossing her arms.

Ryder once again had to push the two apart, but doing so he basically shoved them both in the chest and while Ainsley went stumbling backwards, Ryder's other hand ended up between Naomi's breasts.

He withdrew quickly, his face flaming, but the earth elemental seemed too busy trying to launch herself at the human across from her to notice. "Asshole," she screamed heatedly and he chuckled darkly.

"Like I haven't heard that before."

"That's enough," Sam snapped. "Ainsley, you're with Veronica. Naomi with Marina and Ryder with me."

Marina looped her hand through Naomi's and walked her away, while the taller blonde grabbed Ainsley by the ear and dragged him along whining behind her.

"Don't mind them," Sam said, taking Ryder by the shoulder and leading him in the opposite direction.

"Why do they hate each other that much? I mean Ainsley told me the physical reason but I still don't quite understand how such a wedge could be driven between them." Sam grinned down at him.

"I see we have a poet." Ryder chuckled slightly.

"Sorry – it's kind of how we have to talk in... my world."

"I'm glad you're away from it now," he said sincerely. Sam was taller than Ryder and he guessed maybe even more than Una. He had wavy black hair and honey coloured eyes that were almost gold.

Ryder found himself staring and quickly snapped out of his stupor. "Anyway, they hate each other because that's all they know how to do. I don't think they can imagine a time where they weren't going for each other's throats and maybe they're even afraid of it. It's become a part of their lives now and I think it might be one of those things that can't really be fixed."

"Who's the poet now," Ryder snorted. Sam huffed slightly with a smile and Ryder smiled back.

He could get used to this whole... friends thing.

Then he suddenly stopped.

"Mark!" he slapped his forehead with a groan. "Oh no."

"What? Who's Mark?"

"It doesn't matter." Ryder groaned again and slapped his palm against his forehead a few more times. "Stupid, stupid, stupid!" he whipped around to face Sam once again. "Did you find a bag lying next to me when you found me?"

"I-I don't know, Loch Ness was the one that saved you," Sam said, now worried. "Why, was it important?"

He growled in anger and tugged at his hair. "Fuck," he swore loudly, dropping to the floor and leaning against the wall.

"What's wrong? Do I need to call Loch Ness?"

"You can't, she's in the Dead Zone – whatever that is." Ryder ran a hand over his face and cursed again.

"Hey, if you tell me what's going on I might be able to help."

"The night Loch Ness found me, my mum and I were going to be transferred to Hong Kong central. I went out to see my friend Mark before we left, but then I was attacked. I had a bag with me with plans that we made together and with our DNA all over it. If the government finds it, Mark's dead."

"Plans? What were the plans for?" Ryder hung his head low.

"I-I can't... I can't tell you."

"Well if it's threatening your friend's life – I'd say it's pretty important. In what way were these plans tied to the government?" Sam leaned down in front of him with his elbows leaning on his knees.

Ryder shook his head.

Sam sighed, "Alright. Just try to forget about it for the moment, it should be okay. Loch Ness isn't known for making many mistakes in her missions, I think it's safe to say she's already got your bag."

"Can we look in her room?" Sam seemed slightly taken aback.

"Uh, well – you'd need a key."

Ryder reached into the pocket of his sweats and showed Sam the gleaming silver pebble.

"How on Earth did you get that?"

"Zachary gave it to me so I could get some sort of medicine from her room but I think he forgot I still have it." He put it back in his pocket. "So can we go check?"

"Well I mean – isn't it kinda rude to go snooping around in someone's room?"

"I'm sure Loch Ness would understand if it concerns my friend's life," Ryder argued.

"But –" Sam stopped. "Argh – okay fine. But we go in five minutes then we go out. I'm only doing letting you do this because you said someone might die."

Ryder grinned and the two took off towards Loch Ness's room.

Ryder unlocked it and stepped inside, holding the door open for Sam.

He didn't budge.

"Sam?"

"I never said I was going in there. You have the key, it's your bag and it was your idea to snoop around."

"You said 'we!'"

"Never said I was going inside," he shrugged and Ryder growled.

"Okay fine."

"Tick tock," Sam warned and Ryder dashed inside.

He went scuttling up and down the shelves, peering under the bedsheets and almost hitting his head on the table as he tried to crawl out from underneath it.

"Two minutes," Sam called.

He went into the starry room.

Ryder searched all of the shelves and found himself instinctively keeping his hands away from everything and maneuvering carefully around the glass case in the middle of the room.

"One minute!" He heard the faraway yell and cursed, hurriedly rushing out and peering around the green and black painted door.

The massive glass jar with the raging red liquid was calmer now and simply sloshed slightly against the glass as Ryder eased himself carefully into the room.

He almost stepped on a plant that was growing out the floor and tensed, gripping the edge of the table so tightly he could almost feel his bones cracking.

He didn't dare step any further, but stood on the tips of his toes and leaned as far forward as he could to peer around the room.

"Nothing," he grumbled, then stepped back.

He heard the crunch of a plant beneath his feet and the plant screamed.

He leapt backwards and hit his head on the doorframe – cursed – slammed the door shut and ran outside.

"Twenty-eight –" he slammed into Sam and almost knocked him off his feet. "You still had twenty-seven seconds," Sam said and Ryder gasped for breath, gripping his arm tightly.

"The plant," he gasped. "The plant screamed."

"You went into Loch Ness's garden?"

"Garden!?"

"Look it doesn't matter. You didn't find whatever you were looking for so let's go back."

"Back where?"

"To the training room."

"Why?" Sam rolled his eyes.

"I only took you away so you wouldn't hear Ainsley and Naomi screaming at each other after Veronica and Marina straightened them out. It should technically be safe now. Besides, you still need to meet James."

"What's he like?" Ryder asked as they began walking back. He smiled.

"I think you'll like him."

Truth be told, Ryder was a little intimidated when he saw James.

The massive Scottish man with curly red hair like Mike's and red stubble dotting his jaw loomed over Ryder a good foot above him.

He had twinkling blue eyes and a kind smile that eased Ryder's nerves instantly.

"Ryder – meet the muscle of the team." Veronica introduced.

"Wow, I couldn't tell," Ryder chuckled, shaking the man's hand. James' hand was rather... large in Ryder's and his bicep was nearly the size of his head.

"Pleasure to meet you, Ryder." He had a slight Scottish accent and by the way he talked and acted Ryder could already tell he was a complete gentleman.

"Heyy me nams Jams," Mike slurred from behind Veronica and she cuffed him around the ear again.

James' expression darkened, but he didn't tense up or make any move towards the snickering Scottish boy.

"Are you two siblings?" Ryder asked quietly.

James let out a booming laugh that could have shaken the whole mountain and Ryder's eyes went wide.

"Me and this thing? Related?" he cackled again.

"I take offence to that," Mike huffed in Ryder's direction.

"If this thing was in my family I probably would've pushed him off a cliff," James said, ruffling Michael's hair.

Ryder assumed it was something the team did a lot, because he screeched like his hair was on fire and punched James repeatedly in the stomach until he let go.

"Ryder?" his head jerked up with a startled hum in response and Marina frowned at him. "You okay?"

"Huh? What – yeah. Just a little tired that's all."

Turned out that was the wrong thing to say.

"What!? Do you need to lie down? Do you feel warm? Weak? Dizzy?" Naomi put a hand on his forehead.

"Does this happen often?" Marina asked worriedly and Ainsley nodded.

"Yeah, he almost blew me up once."

"What do you mean he blew you up?" Marina screeched.

"Guys! Stop! I'm fine, honestly. I'm just tired as in mentally tired. There's been a lot of stuff happening these past few days and I just need time to adjust, that's all."

Marina gave him a sceptical look. Naomi looked like she didn't believe him. Ainsley was a safe distance away. Sam had an eyebrow raised at him and Veronica had a hand on her hip that was jutted out with attitude.

"I swear!" he added.

"Fine. But if you feel anything at all, you tell me and I'm taking you to Zachary."

"Overprotective much?" Ainsley muttered. Naomi glared and just like that they were arguing again. Sam groaned and Veronica yanked them apart.

"Can you two stop going at each other for two seconds!?" she yelled.

It was then that Scott materialised a few metres away from them, whipped around in a panic and waved frantically at them.

He dashed over, face grim and eyes blazing. "Senior team two just returned."

"What's wrong?" Sam asked quickly, immediately switching from a calm, boyish student into a solider.

"Only two of them made it back and they're both badly wounded."

"Where are the other three? Dead?" Veronica snapped, quickly striding over.

"Alpha has them."

"We need to contact Loch Ness," Naomi said quickly.

"She's in the Dead Zone," Sam said before Ryder could. "We can't contact her even if we want to."

"Una's already been notified, she sent me to get the senior team. Ryder, you're coming with us too – Naomi and Ainsley have to stay behind."

Sam nodded to Veronica, who nodded back and then Sam curled his fists so his fingers touched the two small silver discs in each palm, then he dematerialised with Scott following suit.

Marina gave Ryder a nod, then both she and James disappeared.

"Do I come too?" Natalie asked quietly and Veronica gave her a small smile.

"No – your job is to make sure everyone stays calm and safe. Make sure nobody panics and we'll take care of the rest."

"Okay," she whispered and Veronica grabbed Ryder's wrist. She grimaced slightly, "Try not to scream, throw up or pass out please."

Then he saw his body disappearing before his eyes, glitching out of existence and the world swam in his vision.

His feet were then suddenly on solid ground once again and he stumbled to his knees, but Veronica thankfully yanked him to his feet before he could hit the floor. He opened his mouth to thank her, but he was abruptly tugged straight up a flight of stairs with his wrist still firmly in her grasp.

"Why can't we just teleport there?" he panted as they rounded a corner.

"Loch Ness designs the security systems on both the teleportation units and certain rooms in the academy. These rooms are off limits so people can't get int them without using brute force."

"Useful for invasions," he joked. Veronica eyed him for a moment, before her eyes flicked back to the direction they were sprinting, her boots thudding against the floor.

His eyes went wide.

"Oh my god are we –"

"Hush." She ripped open the door and Ryder found all four advisors, the rest of Loch Ness's team and a few other people he didn't recognise, already standing in the room.

Una looked positively livid and as soon as he walked through the door he could almost feel her rage crackling in the air.

"How did Alpha manage to defeat three of our best seniors?" she said calmly, her anger evident hiding behind her voice – creeping up into her throat and clutching onto her words like a barnacle.

"The only elementals that escaped were the water and fire elementals," Jarred spoke up. "From the burns on their bodies, I'd say that Alpha has a fire elemental on her hands."

"An elemental!?" Una roared.

Her fists slammed into the wooden desk beneath her palms and the wood cracked, shattering beneath her hands.

When her head snapped up, Ryder saw that her ice blue eyes were now a bright dazzling white.

Everyone in the room flinched back from her display of raw power.

She stood back and flexed her hands, rubbing her left wrist with her right hand.

Everyone waited for her to continue talking – stunned into a fearful silence.

"One of my elementals is on her side?" She asked in a low voice that was chillingly cold.

"We have reason to believe she has more than one," Scott said quietly.

"How many?" she asked, coking her head to the side.

"We can't know for sure until the other two elementals wake up."

"Damnit, where is Loch Ness when I need her," Una snarled. "Contact her with a constant signal – tell her to get here as soon as possible."

"But My Lady, it would take a day at most for the message to reach her and at least three for her to get back here," one of the female advisors said worriedly.

"I don't care," she quipped. "Contact her now, and tell Meredith and Marcus to get back here as soon as possible too."

"But My Lady –"

"I said – I don't care. Get it done." Then she began walking towards the door. "Scott and Jarred, gather up everyone that knows Ryder and if possible, as many of those who've seen him before or gotten a good look at him at least." She pointed to Scott as she spoke, then to the group of people Ryder didn't recognise. "Senior team three – you help him. Senior team one, try to contact Loch Ness with Talia and Hannah." She pointed to the two female advisors and the whole of the team nodded in sync. "Go into her room and get me one of her helmets – one should be on her desk. Zachary has her spare key.

"Ryder, you're with me." He gave Sam a wide-eyed look, who jerked his head in her direction, before turning to stride over to his team.

Ryder grabbed his arm to stop him and he turned around with his mouth open to speak, but Ryder pushed the metal pebble into his palm and closed his fingers over it with a meaningful look. Sam's eyes glittered with understanding and he mouthed a thank you, before walking back over to his team.

Then Ryder dashed after Una.

"Why do you need me?" he asked, but she didn't answer him. He struggled to keep up with her fast strides. "Why did you ask Scott to find anyone who knew me?"

"I don't have time to tell you," she said firmly. His eyes flashed.

"I have every right to know! It's about me and I need to know what to do to help!"

"You can't help. Right now you need to shut up and follow orders."

His anger rose and he ran in front of her and planted his feet into the ground firmly in front of her.

She stopped and looked up at him with gleaming blue eyes.

"Why are you like this?" he said angrily. "Why are you so cold towards everyone? Why do you have to order everyone around without any explanation?"

"Do you want to die?" she asked instead of answering him.

"What?"

"Do you want Loch Ness to die? Do you want those two elementals in Zachary's care to die? Do you want everyone in this academy to be killed?"

"What!? No!"

"Then stop wasting my time. If you're not fast and efficient, you lag behind and you get killed. We are all prey in this game and there's always, always a bigger fish. So if you don't want to become dead prey, I suggest you obey my orders just like everyone else. I didn't become leader by choice. Alpha killed my mother and sibling and led the battle that killed my father. If she isn't stopped, she'll kill everyone I even remotely care about.

"Those three elementals were killed on purpose. I know they're dead. It's in the rules. Three dead elementals means three strokes of the clock – which means war." She leaned closer with a cold look.

"You're part of the game – I see it now. Loch Ness saw it and so did Naomi. You're in the spider's sticky strands now and Alpha just shook the whole web. All the spiders are coming out and if you don't pull the right strands you'll die. I've been in the web far longer than you have and I know the name of the game. So unless you have any more useless insults to throw at me, we should get back to work, don't you think? Or do I need the almighty Ryder's permission?" He lowered his head.

"No, My Lady," he whispered.

She nodded in satisfaction.

"Good." She strode around him and he followed her quickly and silently, keeping his head down.

He did it out of pure fear and guilt for what he'd said.

They reached the end of the hall and she took his wrist, then without warning, they were being thrown through empty space, then he was falling towards the floor.

Una's arm wrapped right around his waist and caught him in one smooth action, delicately lifting back up into a standing position. "Careful," she said, then continued walking forward.

She reached the door with the empty circle and she reached down and slid a large golden bangle off her wrist.

She placed it into the carved out edge of the circle and it slotted easily into place, turning into liquid gold that swirled slowly around the circle.

She pushed the door open and beckoned him inside. He opened his mouth but quickly shut it before Una could turn and see.

"What is it?" She asked and he froze. She didn't turn to look at him, instead, walking over to the shelves that lined the walls just like Loch Ness's room. "You have a question."

"Why is your security so simple compared to Loch Ness's?"

"It's not," she said simply, bringing out a scroll and unravelling it, before rolling it back up and sliding it back into the shelves. "There is only one key and I keep it on me at all times. It will turn to liquid gold for anyone else who tries to hold it. It stays solid only for someone with royal blood." He nodded solemnly and watched her bring out more scrolls. "No, I'm afraid I can't tell you what I'm looking for," she said softly – out of the blue.

What is she, a mind reader?

"No," she said, amused. She turned to him with a small smirk on her lips. "I can hear thoughts though. With training, people can hide their thoughts from me, as I can only hear their minds whispering to me."

She took out another scroll.

"Your mind is very loud and complex. With you, I can hear your thoughts, but also see them on your face. Occasionally, I can even feel them."

"Wow," he blurted.

"Naomi has a gift such as mine," Una continued and Ryder stayed silent, afraid that if he spoke she would stop and be silent for the rest of the time he was there. "She knows when people are in trouble, when they are hurt. She can see it in their eyes and even feel it from miles away."

"Feel it?" he asked before he could stop himself.

"She describes it as a tingling feeling," Una said offhandedly as her eyes skimmed over the scroll's contents, her finger following each and every word as she read it. "A warm tremor that starts in her fingers and makes its way into the palms of her hands. She's remarkable."

"Truly," Ryder said, trying to push her into saying more.

"But then there's Loch Ness. She can tell apart even the slightest of lies and she can see you. Really, see you." She shook her head and rolled the parchment back up. "I wonder what happened to make her as distant as I." Ryder decided to take advantage of her good nature in the moment.

"Why didn't everyone else follow us when we left?"

"They needed to discuss and plan before they sprung into action," she said with a smile directed at him. "Unlike you, some people like to think about what they're doing before they do it. Such as a misdirected punch at an enemy. An unplanned swipe of a paintbrush. Or even... breaking into someone's room."

He stiffened immediately, his jaw now wide open, but she didn't even turn to meet his startled gaze.

She took out yet another scroll. "It's got to be here somewhere," she muttered to herself and Ryder gathered up the courage to stutter out,

"What do you mean by that?" She turned around, innocent.

"By what?"

He narrowed her eyes – what she had said before was true. She was a master of the game and she knew exactly what she was doing to him.

"I'm not going to play your game," he muttered and she raised an eyebrow.

"So you did break into Loch Ness's room?"

"When did I say that!?" he shrieked. She laughed and Ryder was swept away by the sincerity of it.

"You are very amusing, you know?" she said with a sideways glance and a bright smile.

He shrugged, a little flustered.

"If you say so, My Lady." She laughed again.

"Whoa, so modest!"

His lips lifted up into a smile as she turned back around and he froze.

Am I falling for her?

So he quickly caught himself before he did, pinching his lips shut and staring at the floor as the woman searched through the scrolls on the shelves.

He was not going to fall for the queen of the Kediotherylan realm.

Chapter 6

"The signal's been sent out, but it hasn't reached her yet," Veronica said as soon as she walked through the door that Ryder opened for her.

Una was at her desk, skimming over a few scrolls at a time.

"We just got one of her helmets too," Sam said, handing the spiked black helmet to his leader. She took it with a nod of thanks.

She flicked up the visor which unlocked something else with a click, then she tugged on the part near the chin, which slid up completely, showing an open, padded space that would usually go around the back of Loch Ness's head.

It had a round space near the top around the size of Ryder's fist, so he guessed Loch Ness had her hair in a bun when she wore it.

Una slid the helmet on and clicked the top piece into place so they could only see her ice blue eyes, then she flicked down the visor.

She didn't move at all for a few seconds and Ryder opened his mouth to ask what she was doing, but Veronica slapped a hand over his mouth.

After a few more tense seconds of silence, she unlocked the helmet and slid it back off again with a smile.

"I don't know how, but she already knew that we needed her here. She's already on her way back."

"But the signal hasn't reached her yet, I checked," Marina said in confusion, showing Una the glass panel she held in her hands.

The queen grinned predatorily.

It seemed to be the only way that she could smile.

"I think I know how."

"How!?" Sam burst, throwing his hands up.

"I'll be back – I need her key." Sam threw it to her and she caught it with a swipe of her palm so quickly Ryder thought she'd just slapped it halfway across the room.

Then she left.

She came back a moment later with a massive jar that Ryder definitely found familiar. "Wha!?" he managed to force out, but Una placed the jar on the desk and unscrewed the top.

Ryder soon realised that the liquid couldn't just move – but it was sentient.

Unlike a normal liquid, this one was thicker, more like slime than anything else.

It slid out and sat on her paper without damaging them at all, blowing bubbles at her and making its surface ripple.

"Can you contact Loch Ness for me?" Una asked politely. It leaned away from her and slithered off her table, landing on the floor with a splat, before slowly crawling around the room, circling each and every person – assessing them.

Then it began climbing up the wall.

Once it got to around eye level, it stretched itself out into a circle that covered most of the shelves.

Its body then began changing colours until a picture formed in hues of red.

"Loch Ness?" Una called out, leaning closer.

The figure being showed was completely red except for their helmet which was the darkest hue of burgundy the slime could manage.

The figure waved at everyone and Ryder stared with wide eyes.

"How is that even possible!?"

"Loch Ness, can you hear me?" The figure tapped the side of their helmet, then pointed to Una and shook her head. "She can't hear any of us and we can't hear her. I'm guessing this creature only has the ability to share live footage and not sound," Una said with a smile. She turned back to the weird circle of red slime and showed it her watch, then tapped it while looking at the figure.

They nodded with a salute, then the liquid bubbled and returned to its original shade of red.

It slowly folded back in on itself and slithered down the wall, then hopped into the jar and screwed it closed.

It happily bubbled at everyone, slowly lapping against the edges of the glass.

"It knew how to get in and out this entire time?" Ryder gaped.

A small tentacle came out of the blob and turned to him, nodded, then shrunk back.

Sam laughed. "Seems like it understands far more than just where Loch Ness is too."

"She'll be back here in a few days, until then, we need to do the best we can to help find all the people that know Ryder, and to get the two elementals on their way towards recovery. Ryder, can you put the jar back in Loch Ness's room?" She grinned. "I'm sure you know where it goes."

He stuttered slightly, then clamped his lips shut and nodded, took the jar stiffly and wandered back out the door with the silver pebble balanced on top of the jar.

He walked into her room and opened the door to what Sam called a 'garden,' but what looked more like an abandoned room that had been left to be taken over by nature.

...Which was probably what actually happened.

Ryder carefully placed the jar on the table with a sigh, before slowly trying to back out of the room.

It was then that he noticed the small green plant behind him that was only a tiny shoot, with two crushed leaves that had been smeared onto the wooden planks beneath it.

He winced, crouching down to examine it.

"Sorry," he muttered to it, reaching down and carefully peeling the leaves off the floorboards and trying to get it to stand upright.

He let go and it leaned over to slump on the floorboards again.

He squeaked and quickly tried to make it stand again.

It continued to slump over.

"Uh, just wait a second..." He went out to the main room and made sure the door was closed, then put his hand next to the hole on the other side of the lock.

The metal pebble was sucked into his hand, locking the door, then he pocketed it and walked back into the indoor garden.

He saw a small stream of water trickling down the wall at the back and slowly walked over, crisscrossing through the room while trying not to step on any of the plants.

He reached it and cupped his hands underneath the small trickle, before rushing as fast as he could back to the plant and letting the water drip over it.

It seemed to perk up slightly.

"Hopefully that helps," he muttered to himself with a small smile.

There was a small creak as the lid of the jar unscrewed again and the slime crawled out and bubbled along the floor.

"Hello –" he squeaked and froze as it began clambering up his pant leg.

It felt warm through the fabric and as it slid over his legs he squirmed and sucked in a terrified breath.

It got to his shoulder and he screwed his eyes shut.

It then began sliding down his arm and swarmed over his right hand.

He let out the breath he was holding. "Oh, is that all you – AHH!" he screamed as his hand was yanked to the side and he desperately tried not to step on any of the plants as he was yanked over to the shelves.

The red slime guided his hand to a small bottle of silvery-grey liquid and clamped around it, before walking Ryder back over to the plant. It then split in two and its other half went along his arm to the other hand, before guiding Ryder to uncork the bottle and drip a single drop onto the leaves of the plant.

It then dragged him backwards with immense speed and not a second later, the plant shot right out of the floorboards and grew up to Ryder's ribcage, new leaves sprouting and bark forming on its trunk.

It was small, but had a massive black flower, and it bloomed, then curled back in on itself within a few seconds, then began bulging outwards.

Ryder took a wary step back.

It bulged to almost thrice its original size until it looked more like a volleyball than anything else.

Then the petals snapped back like a rubber band and sitting – no – levitating in front of the middle of the flower was a volleyball-sized sphere of roiling, glittering gold.

"Wow..." He reached out to touch it, but the red slime was still all over his hands and it quickly tugged him away. "Why can't I touch it?"

A tentacle waved at him from his left hand, shaking from side to side as if it was waggling a finger at him. "Okay..." He stepped back and sat down on a chair, watching the flower petals dance around the floating ball of golden light.

He watched it for what seemed like seconds, but when he finally looked down at his watch, he realised it was almost four in the afternoon.

He quickly leapt to his feet and dashed out of the room, skidding to a stop and rushing back again to put the small vial of silver liquid back on the shelf before he ran back out again, being careful not to touch the roiling ball of gold.

Ryder pushed the pebble into the lock, opened it, ran out and collected it from the opposite side of the lock, then ran into the medical room.

When he burst in, Zachary looked up from the glass pane in his hand with wide eyes. "Oh, it's just you," he sighed, walking over. He suddenly stopped and eyed Ryder's hands. "Or not just you."

Ryder looked down and saw the red slime still covering both his hands.

"Fascinating," Zachary murmured. "Is it one of Loch Ness's inventions?" The slime seemed offended and reached out a tentacle to wiggle angrily at him. "Oh my – it's sentient, isn't it? Remarkable..."

"Yeah very remarkable – now can you please hold it while I go to the toilet?" He put his hands in front of Zachary, but when he tried to touch the slime, it slid right up his arms in a frenzy, ending up sitting in his hair and hissing threateningly. "Come on, it's just for a little bit," Ryder groaned.

It seemed to fuse to his head in response, dripping slightly down his forehead and bubbling happily.

He groaned. "You know what, forget it. I'll be back in a sec," he said to Zach, running to the bathroom.

The slime was actually surprisingly obedient and simply sat in his hair until he washed his hands, at which point it seemed to want to play in the water because it leapt right off his head and slapped onto the sink will a shrill squeak of happiness.

Water shot out the sides of the sink and Ryder flinched back, covering his face as it drenched him.

The slime happily milled around the sink, letting the water flow over its body as it splashed around with its multiple tentacles. Ryder laughed. "You're like a little kid," he mused aloud, picking it up.

It wrapped around his entire right arm, stretching out until it covered his entire arm and hand like a massive glove.

He smiled and turned off the tap before he walked out of the bathroom.

"Having fun in there?" Zachary asked and Ryder rolled his eyes.

"Hey, do you know what species this is?"

"No clue. Never seen it before in my life," the medic answered, scratching the back of his neck thoughtfully.

"It can... show images?" Ryder tried to explain. Zachary looked over at him.

"What do you mean by that, exactly?"

"Uhhh... Well um, I guess can ask it to show you??" He lifted his arm and stared at it. "Um, can you... show me Loch Ness please?"

It slid under his shirt and he felt it nestle under his armpit, gurgling in a way he hadn't heard before.

It sounded a little like a warning growl – the kind that a dog made when it heard something rustling in the bushes behind the windows before it let out a full on bark.

"I don't think it likes you," Ryder said simply to Zach and he frowned.

"Alright. Well, I could use a helping hand... would you mind?"

"Oh, no of course not – what do you need?"

"Well, first you should see the two elementals that came back from a mission to Alpha's base."

Zachary led Ryder to a secluded room on the other side of the medical room and showed him to the two metal tables.

The two figures were levitating over the medical tables with the same blue grids holding them up like when Ryder got his scan.

They were in pale lilac hospital gowns and neither of them were moving.

"They're unstable at the moment," Zach said quietly, tapping away on the pane in his hand once again. "Both had more than seventy-five percent of their energy sucked out of them."

"Is that bad?" Ryder asked.

"Less than fifty percent isn't ideal, and if an elemental's levels are below twenty-five percent they are taken off the battlefield imme-diately. It's a rule. Below twenty and they go unconscious. Anyone that's gone below ten has died. That's why we need Loch Ness and fast – their levels are already below fourteen."

"Their energy can be replenished – right?" He sighed, walking over to the male and lifting up the gown to look at the burns all over his chest.

"Usually. The low it gets, the slower it replenishes. If it doesn't get to a stable level quickly enough, it will start to decrease and they'll die."

"Can I see their energy scans?" Zachary tapped on the screen and handed it to him.

"The one on the left is the male. He's a twenty-seven-year-old water elemental. The one on the right is the female – a thirty-four-year-old fire elemental. You can swipe to the right to see an average elemental's levels." Zachary then walked over to the shelves and began pulling bottles off and muttering to himself.

Ryder flicked to the other screen and zoomed in on the scan.

The three balls of golden light he's seen on the human scan previously were much larger on the elemental's screen – instead of pea-sized, it was more tennis-ball sized.

He thought back to his own scan and realised why Loch Ness was so concerned.

He pushed it out of his mind.

He flicked back to the previous scans and zoomed in on the female's energy scan.

Her energy was almost non-existent.

He stared at the golden ball of light that pulsed in the middle of her chest and squinted at it.

"Hey Zach, I'll be back in a sec, okay?"

"Where are you going?" Ryder paused at the door to answer him.

"Loch Ness's room, need anything from there?"

"Why are you going back? You were in there for hours."

"Just... I'll be back, alright?" He dashed out.

As soon as he got back in the garden-room, the black flower turned its head towards him, the glowing ball of golden light pulsing and turning slowly.

"Can you please contact Loch Ness?" he asked the slime that was now once again sitting in his hair.

It slowly slid off his arm and jumped onto the wall, spreading out and morphing into an image.

Loch Ness's spiked helmet came into view. She cocked her head to the side and Ryder ran out of the room with a yelled, "Stay there, okay??" He rummaged through her desk for a pen and paper, finding a strange glass pane just like Zachary had.

He tapped it and two dots appeared on the screen.

He quickly wrote a message with his finger and ran back inside, holding it up to the slime.

How far away are you?

Loch Ness turned away from him to face a different direction and the image swayed slightly, like she was going around a corner.

She looked back again and on her visor, a blinking light started typing across it.

Around a day. I'm swimming as fast as I can.

He used his fist to rub out the message and wrote another.

Swimming?

She responded instantly.

The Dead Zone is inside the Dead Sea. It's completely underwater.

He wrote again, a long message that Loch Ness waited patiently for until he held the glass pane back up again.

This weird slime thing poured a silver liquid on a plant and it grew this weird golden ball of light. It looks like the energy spheres I saw on the scans.

Loch Ness's response came instantaneously.

Don't touch it.

I didn't, don't worry, the slime thing stopped me.

He paused.

What is it?

The slime or the plant?

The plant.

It's just a normal plant that you can find in this realm. It has massive reserves of energy, so I tested my invention on it first.

The message disappeared and appeared quickly and Ryder's eyes skimmed across them as fast as he could,

I created a solution from Una's blood that can extract the energy from the plant. This means that we can grow and harvest energy to give to wounded elementals.

He wrote so quickly his words were all jumbled up, but Loch Ness seemed to be able to read it as he held it up.

We can use it to heal the two elementals that came back from Alpha's base, right?

No. The energy is impure, it's dangerous and I'm still trying to study it. Make sure you don't touch the energy or the plant until I get back.

He nodded to show he understood.

No more messages showed for a moment.

Find the helmet Una used and put it on. Malarackthyr – can you connect us?

The slime bubbled in response.

"Mala-what now?" Ryder asked, baffled, turning to the slime. "And you can read!?"

Loch Ness tapped her helmet, then the image disappeared.

Ryder fetched the helmet and flicked up the visor like Una had, then yanked on the bottom of the helmet.

It slid up easily and he put it on, clicked the first part into place, then flicked down the visor.

He could see everything clearly through the visor as if he was looking through pristine glass.

He watched as the slime wandered up his arm and sat on top of the helmet, sitting on the spikes without any harm to it at all.

Then images began flashing on the visor in front of him.

Suddenly he was staring into a pair of hazel brown eyes.

"Loch Ness?" he spoke. The skin around their eyes was slightly tanned, but curling around their left eye was mottled red skin.

"I'm out of the Dead Zone now – which means you can contact me through Malarackthyr." She said instantly, her eyes flicking to something in front of her.

"It's been very useful," Ryder remarked.

"He is, isn't he?"

"He??" Ryder said, baffled.

"At the moment," she said breezily. "Can you take me to the medical room?" He nodded and walked out of her room and towards Zachary.

"What the hell are you doing wearing –"

"Hello, Zachary," Loch Ness spoke and this time her voice came from both inside and outside the helmet.

Zach's eyes went wide.

"You're out of the Dead Zone?"

"Just. Can you show me the elementals?"

Ryder stood in front of the two tables acting as a transmitter as Zachary began using complex terms to describe what was going on that he didn't understand, but Loch Ness seemed to.

"From what you've told me, they don't have much time left. I can either come back as fast as I can and risk going under once I get back, or get there too late."

Zachary's eyes flicked to his patients.

"Don't risk it – you're the only one who can fix this."

"I've already calculated what speed to go at to maximise their chances," Loch Ness prodded. "If I go fast enough to get there on time, but slow enough so as not to push me off the edge, I might be able to save them." Zachary looked torn. He turned to Ryder with wide eyes.

"Do it," Ryder said.

"Why!?" Zachary burst out.

"She knows what she's doing. From what I've heard, Una trusts her more than she does her own advisors and teachers. She must have had to earn that trust. She can do this." Zachary looked close to tugging his hair out.

"Okay fine. Get back here in one piece please."

"Will do," Loch Ness said quietly, then her eyes flicked to Ryder on the inside of the visor before they faded out and the quiet whirring in the helmet went silent.

He took it off and looked to Zachary, who looked deep in thought. What do we do now?"

"Nothing," he said simply. "Now, all we can do it wait."

Loch Ness returned to the academy early the next morning and as soon as she stumbled out of the flying capsule, she collapsed.

Zachary carried her all the way to the medical room and set her down on the floor, to which Ryder began protesting until he realised why.

She crossed her legs and sat up straight, then placed her palms on her knees and went still.

She was lifted a few centimetres off the floor so she was levitating, but the only other movement she made was the rise and fall of her chest and shoulders as she breathed.

"She's doing quiet energy preservation," Zachary told Ryder.

"What's that?"

"A few very skilled students can force themselves into a coma and shut down all their functions except for the necessary ones and speed up their energy replenishing process."

She sat there for hours and Ryder sat by her side, only getting up for lunch and to go to the bathroom.

It was just after dinner when she suddenly leapt to her feet and ran out of the room.

Ryder, who was just about dozing off – scrambled to his feet and ran after her.

Malarackthyr had taken to sitting happily on Loch Ness's helmet – it seemed to have a very strong bond with his companion – and quite happily continued sitting there as she dashed into her room.

Ryder followed her best he could and found that she had gone immediately into the garden-room.

She was looking at the plant in fascination, and it had turned its withered black petals towards her, the golden light bulging outwards – as if trying to reach her.

"Fascinating," she murmured.

She went over to the desk connected to the wall and pulled out a bunch of notebooks, muttering to herself.

Ryder stood quietly, only moving to get out of the way when she walked past him into the main room.

At one point she opened a door on the left side of the room and Ryder peered inside to find it led directly to the other room – the inventive room.

"Why do you have two separate... uh..." he asked when she came back with an axe and a... rock?

"Offices," she inputted. "They represent two sides of me – the doctor and the scientist. A bit of both my parents I suppose."

"Your parents?"

"Abandoned me once they saw my scarred face," she said with a grunt, yanking half the blade of the axe off and Ryder jumped. "They're no parents of mine."

"Anything I can do to help?" He asked and she turned to him. "With what you're doing, I mean," he said quickly.

"Don't touch the flower or the ball of energy," she repeated. "Oh, and keep Michael out if he tries to come in please, he's rather distracting."

"He's n—"

There was a banging on the door.

Ryder gave Loch Ness a wide-eyed look, but she was too busy muttering to herself and scribbling things into a notebook to notice his stare.

He walked into the main room and opened the door.

There was a flash of red as the boy tried to dash into the room, but Ryder caught him by the back of his collar. "Whoa, whoa, whoa – where do you think you're going?"

"To see Loch Ness!" He said, ripping himself out of Ryder's grip.

He grabbed the boy around the waist, carried him outside and plopped him down on the other side of the door. "She's busy."

"I don't care!"

"Well, I do."

"She wants to see me!"

"She specifically told me to keep you away." He gasped.

"She did not –"

"Michael, I'm working on something very important right now, so can you please listen to Ryder," Loch Ness called from the other room.

The boy scowled.

"Okay fine. Can I stay in here?"

"No," Ryder sighed, pushing him back out again. "You're too distracting."

"I am not!"

"Now you're both being distracting," Loch Ness growled. "Ryder, can you please take Mike out? Michael – listen to Ryder please and don't kill anyone. Come back in an hour."

"But –"

"There are people dying, Michael."

The two males glared at each other, but obeyed, closing the door behind them and setting off down the hallway – neither of them knowing where they were going.